Micah moved toward the door, which Rachel was starting to close. "Wait—" he said. "I want to help you."

"Oh, that's rich," she said. "Just how are you going to do that?" She turned away from him.

"Look, I know I don't deserve your forgiveness," he said.

"No, you don't," she agreed, lifting her chin.

He stopped in front of her, lifted a hand. "Rachel..."

"Go," she whispered on a ragged breath. "Just go."

Micah stepped onto the porch, and she closed the screen door. He stood there facing the sun that burned into his eyes, his fingertips in his jeans pockets. Finally he cleared his throat. "You have no idea how much I regret what I did to you," he said.

But she was already gone.

Books by Sharon Mignerey

Love Inspired Suspense

Through the Fire #17
Small Town Secrets #22
Shadows of Truth #45

SHARON MIGNEREY

After living most of her life in Colorado, Sharon recently moved to the Texas Gulf coast, where Southern hospitality lives up to its reputation for being warm and welcoming. She wanted to be a storyteller since she learned that spelling words could be turned into stories. Sharon's first book was published in 1997 after winning RWA's Golden Heart Award in 1995. That same book went on to win the National Reader's Choice Award. In addition to writing novels, Sharon has had several articles published by *The Writer Magazine*. She says the accolades are wonderful, but the only lasting satisfaction comes from serving the work. When she's not writing, you can find her being happily involved with her critique group, learning how to garden in the Texan heat or playing with her two rescued shih tzus.

Sharon loves hearing from readers. She can be reached through her Web site www.sharonmignerey.com or in care of Steeple Hill Books, 233 Broadway, Suite 1001, New York, NY 10279.

Shadows of Truth

SHARON MIGNEREY

Steeple
Hill®

Published by Steeple Hill Books™

STEEPLE HILL BOOKS

Steeple
Hill®

ISBN-13: 978-0-373-44235-5
ISBN-10:   0-373-44235-1

SHADOWS OF TRUTH

www.SteepleHill.com

Printed in U.S.A.

Consider my affliction and my travail.
Forgive all my sins.
—*Psalms* 25:18

My deepest gratitude to Barbara Harrison,
Judythe Hixson, Sue Hornick and Pamela Nowak—
you each are amazing lights.

ONE

Busting a gang of drug dealers would be easier than going to the door to ask for Rachel Neesham's forgiveness. Even so, Micah McLeod was back in Carbondale, Colorado, a scant hour's drive from Aspen. Last spring, he had left town to follow a trail of evidence, first to Aspen, then to Cabo San Lucas, all the while pretending his undercover assignment here hadn't rocked his world.

In truth, he had run.

In truth, he wasn't sure he would have come back now if not for the threat he knew was hanging over Rachel's head. That thought shamed him. She had deserved far better from him than he had ever given her.

Taking a deep breath, he opened the wrought-iron gate in front of Rachel's big, two-story Victorian house and stepped onto the brick walkway that led to her front door. He squared his shoulders and climbed the two steps, each scrape of his boot against the wood echoing in his conscience.

The late-afternoon sun burned into his shoulder

blades like a laser. The heavy oak door with its oval etched glass stood open, implying welcome. Once, he had been, and now he hoped she would give him the second chance he had failed to give her.

Her safety depended upon it, though he didn't have hard evidence to prove it. Yet.

A month ago, Rachel's old business partner, Angela London, had started leaving him messages from prison. Since she was a proven liar and a convicted felon, he'd figured she was simply working an angle, and he hadn't been in any hurry to see her. Now, he wished he had answered her summons the first day she had called. The case that had put Angela behind bars had taken one more unpredictable turn, and Rachel was once again caught in the crosshairs.

He frowned, staring into the house beyond the screen door. Given the threats she had received, Rachel should have the house locked up. As it was, anyone could walk right in.

The fragrance from brilliant flowers overflowing the huge terra-cotta pots framing the door assaulted his senses and ratcheted up his unease. Through the screen, the foyer was gilded in sunlight, his own shadow stretching down a hallway that he knew led to the kitchen.

The house always made him think of home, and he realized that was because of the woman and children who lived there. They represented everything he thought a home should be. Welcoming. Generous. Loving. It was like the one he'd grown up in. As an adult, he'd never had that for himself.

He rang the bell, the chimes echoing through the house.

"I'll get it, Mom," a childish voice called, as light footsteps clattered down the stairs that framed one side of the entryway.

Sarah. The seven-year-old who looked so much like her mother. In the next instant she appeared, looking taller than she had last spring. Her honey-colored flyaway hair framed her face like a halo.

"Micah!" The little girl's face lit, and she unlatched the screen door and pushed it open, then skipped forward. "You came back. I kept telling Mom you would. She didn't believe me." She took him by the hand and led him into the house.

He should have turned tail and run while he could. Leaving last spring without even telling Rachel's children goodbye had been nearly as difficult as leaving Rachel. Behind him, the door slammed shut.

"Mom." Sarah pulled him toward the kitchen while his courage fled like a rat. "Look who's here."

A dish towel in her hands, Rachel appeared in the doorway, one of those long skirts she favored swirling around her calves. She looked wonderful...she looked too thin...tired. A half smile curved her lips. When her gaze lit on him, shock and outrage replaced the smile as she gasped.

"You." Her voice was just as cold as he had been afraid it would be.

"Hello, Rachel."

She opened her mouth—to order him out of the house, he was sure—then composed her face into the expressionless mask she'd worn the day he had taken her in for questioning. "Sarah, sweetie, go play with your brother."

"*Mom.*"

"Now." Rachel's tone was as firm as he'd ever heard it.

Last spring when they had first met, Micah hadn't thought her capable of being this stern. Then, she had been his prime suspect, odd as it seemed now, odd as it had been then. An antique dealer with wealthy patrons, providing cover for drug-smuggling and money-laundering, a business owned by two women who had been childhood friends. Neither were the sort of scum he was used to dealing with. He'd been drawn to Rachel's softness, sure it was a facade. He hadn't understood until it was too late what an essential part of her nature that gentleness was.

Sarah let go of his hand and gave him a long considering look before climbing the stairs. Rachel stared at the floor while they both listened to the child's retreating footsteps. The high cheekbones that gave Rachel's face an exotic cast were more pronounced than ever, undoubtedly because she was thinner than she had been last spring.

The month he'd spent ignoring Angela's calls had been a month too long. Oh, he'd told himself that he was too busy, but that would have been only half-true— he was always overworked. The simple truth was, Angela reminded him of Rachel, and thoughts of the awful things he had done to her in the name of his job kept him from sleeping at night. How could he ask for God's forgiveness when he had done the unforgivable?

He studied Rachel's bent head, hating that she looked so drawn, hating that his actions were undoubtedly the cause. The instant Sarah's voice carried to them as she said something to her brother, Rachel lifted her head and advanced on him like a mama bear protecting her young.

"You…" Her finger was pointed at him, carrying every accusation he believed he deserved. "…Turn yourself around and get out of my house right now. You're not welcome here."

"Rachel." This was every bit as bad as he had feared.

"Don't you 'Rachel' me with your sweet voice and your lies."

"I came to…" *Ask for your forgiveness.* Except that he didn't deserve it. "…Explain." True, as far as it went.

"I heard all the explanation I needed at Angela's arraignment, Agent McLeod." Rachel swept past him, the top of her head barely reaching his shoulder, her light-brown hair gleaming in the sunlight as she headed for the front door. "You used me. You lied to me."

"Not intentionally."

"You know that old saying about good intentions paving the road to hell." She held open the door and motioned for him to leave. "You abused my trust." She sucked in a shuddering breath, then stilled while she waited for him, the dish towel clenched so tightly that her knuckles were nearly as white as the cloth.

He slowly walked toward her, wishing she'd look at him. She didn't.

"I had no choice," he said. "The job came first."

"And it still does, doesn't it?" Her eyes finally met his.

Holding her gaze tore a hole inside him. Once he'd thought the luminous green of her eyes contained all the colors of life. Now they were as cloudy and dull as a ruined emerald.

He couldn't give her the outright denial he so wanted to. Striving for as much of the truth as he could manage in this instant, he said, "I heard about the threats and the demand for—"

"Still checking up on me, Agent McLeod?"

"Angela called me after you went to see her." Micah stared at Rachel, echoes of his questioning of her last spring ringing through his head. Then he had still been half convinced Rachel was involved in Angela's criminal activities, and he had threatened her. *I'll be your shadow, Rachel. You won't be able to sneeze without me knowing about it.* That had been a lie, too, since he had left, figuring she'd be better off. And look at where that had gotten her.

Rachel's face paled even more. "I don't have the money."

"I know you don't."

"I don't know where it is."

"I know that, too."

"If you come back, it had better be with a warrant." Once again she motioned toward the door.

"You're not a suspect, Rachel." Reluctantly Micah moved toward it, sure he was about to lose his one chance. Though he was sure she wanted anything from him as much as she wanted a snake bite, he said, "I want to help."

"Oh, that's rich." She let go of the door, and it

slapped closed. Once again she advanced on him, all righteous fury despite the quivering of her chin. "And just how are you going to do that? Are you ready to call on my customers and assure them that I'm not peddling drugs to their children?" She snapped her fingers. "I have it. The bank that called due my loan. It's a little hard to pay back money on a business that isn't *in* business any more. Can you fix that?" When he didn't answer she rushed on. "No, I didn't think so." Her eyes took on a shimmer. "Can you restore my reputation, Agent McLeod?"

"I'm sorry," he said.

"Save it for someone who cares." She turned away from him and again opened the door.

"I know I don't deserve your forgiveness."

"No, you don't," she agreed lifting her chin.

He stopped in front of her, lifted a hand. "Rachel…"

"Go," she whispered, her voice ragged. "Just go."

Micah stepped onto the porch and she closed the screen door. He stood there, his back to the door, his fingertips in his jeans pockets. Finally he cleared his throat and said, "You have no idea how much I regret what I did to you." He raised his head but she was gone, both doors shutting him out. His heart heavy with loss, he turned back around, crossed the porch, and went down the walk.

Away from the woman he hadn't known he loved until after he had ruined her.

From behind the sheer curtains in the parlor, Rachel watched him drive away, her fist pressed against her mouth to keep from crying out. For a single heartbeat, she had been glad to see him because the truth was she missed her friendship with him, grieved for it every bit as much as she grieved for her friendship with Angela. In the next heartbeat she remembered that he hadn't been her friend at all and that she had been his suspect.

You're not a suspect. Did she dare believe him?

The sharp pain of loss filled her all over again. For her best friend who had betrayed her. For her business that she had loved so much and sunk her life savings into. For the dreams that Micah had inspired. For the loss of it all.

"Mom," came Sarah's tentative voice from the doorway.

As she had done so many times over the last few months, Rachel straightened her back and forced the muscles in her face to relax into an expression that hid her grief and her anger.

"Yes, sweetie?" she said, turning around.

Sarah stood uncertainly in the doorway, rubbing her finger against her thumbnail as she often did when she was thinking.

"Why are you so mad at Micah?" she asked.

Rachel weighed that part of the truth she was willing to tell her daughter. She couldn't tell Sarah that she had been falling in love with the man, that for the first time since her husband had died she'd felt alive and young and happy. Sarah wouldn't understand that Micah's friendship had been a sham. How could she? Rachel herself didn't understand it.

Remembering the day she had hired Micah, she stared at her daughter. Never in Rachel's wildest dreams had she imagined the carpenter with his competent hands and his dark, gentle eyes would turn out to be an undercover agent with the DEA, sent to investigate her as a possible drug dealer.

He hadn't been her friend after all, which made her impulse to call him after the threats started all the more stupid.

The first demand for a half-million dollars had come via an e-mail, and she had deleted it, sure it was spam. The next demand had come in the mail, the plain white paper in an equally plain white envelope with no return address containing a single sentence. She'd thrown that away, too, sure that it was an awful prank, playing on all her new vulnerability. Then, a rock had been thrown through the living-room window one night, but the police had dismissed it as a random act of vandalism, probably by neighborhood kids.

Rachel had known it had something to do with the demand for money. She had been so certain of it that she had gone to see Angela in prison. Since she had been convicted of using their business to launder drug money, Rachel assumed the demands had something to do with Angela's old activities. She had told Rachel she didn't know a thing about a missing half-million and Rachel had left the prison that day, sure an overactive imagination had piled on top of her recent catastrophes and made her fear the very worst. She'd decided it all had to be some hideous prank, and that it was perfectly safe to let her children ride their bikes up and down the block without seeing a bogeyman behind every bush.

Rachel's heart pounded as one realization after

another sank into her. Angela had lied…again. The demand for money *wasn't* some outrageous practical joke—it was real. Micah was back, which had to mean she *was* once again a suspect no matter what he said. His nicely put apology had to be merely for show. And somebody wanted money she knew nothing about.

"Mom?" Sarah asked, drawing Rachel's attention away from her bleak thoughts.

"He lied to me," she finally said. "A huge lie that I don't think I can forgive."

"Did he tell you he was sorry?" Sarah asked with the direct logic reserved for the very young.

Rachel nodded.

"Then, you're supposed to forgive him," her daughter said. "That's what Mrs. Berrey says in Sunday school."

It was also the advice of Rachel's father, a retired minister.

If only forgiveness were that simple. Rachel crossed the room to her daughter, gave her a quick hug, and wondered how to answer. From the beginning she had taught her children to live by the lessons passed on to her by her father. At the core of her being she had believed, really believed, in everything she'd learned. Love thy neighbor as thyself. Do unto others as you would have them do unto you. What you ask for in faith shall be given to you. Until last spring, she had been so sure those beliefs were as much a part of her as her next breath.

She'd been wrong. She had played by the rules, had lived the kind of life expected of the daughter of a minister, and she had been happy with it. But as it turned out, faith had been as hollow as promises made by her lifelong friend, Angela. Faith hadn't protected her or her family, and it hadn't provided an iota of comfort.

"If a person says they're sorry, you're supposed to say that it's okay," Sarah said.

"That's very good advice." She brushed Sarah's bangs off her forehead and pressed a kiss there. "But it may take me a while to accept his apology."

"I told you that he'd come back," Sarah said.

"Yes, you did." And each time her daughter had made the prediction, Rachel had prayed she would never see the man again.

More than ever, she knew God had turned a deaf ear to her prayers, a knowledge she had confessed to her dad one bleak night. The deaf ear, he had told her, was hers, not God's. They had argued, and she'd felt battered by the notion that she had abandoned God when it was clearly the other way around.

Over the last few months she had lost nearly everything that had been important to her. Her business. Her reputation. Her ability to provide a comfortable living for herself and her children. Prayer hadn't helped, and the platitudes offered by well-meaning friends cut to the quick. As for God—that serene Presence she'd felt all her life was gone as though it had never been.

She kept that to herself, though.

The last time she had voiced that thought, her dad had told her that life came down to only two choices. Move toward your Source or away from it.

"The reason you don't feel God," he had told her, "is because you've locked your heart up tight, and you've moved away from Him."

"And I came here to talk to my father, hoping he'd understand at least a little bit," she had replied. "Instead, once again, I got the minister, who doesn't understand at all."

That had been a long-standing argument between them, but now it seemed insurmountable. All she wanted was for her dad to comfort her, because she was still just as scared as she'd sometimes been when she was a child. The ensuing rift felt as deep as Glenwood Canyon to Rachel. Now, they no longer spoke except as it related to Sarah and Andy. She wouldn't deny him access to his grandchildren since the three of them were his only living family.

Dragging her thoughts back to the moment, she looked down at Sarah. "Want to help me finish making dinner?"

"Okay."

Rachel forced another smile. "Okay."

And for an hour, she could pretend that making dinner was the biggest challenge she faced.

TWO

The following morning, Rachel headed for work, hearing her father's voice in her head. "Be bold as a lion, Rachel," had been his advice right after Angela's arraignment last spring. "Only the guilty have reason to hide in the dark." Except, she felt guilty, even if only by association.

As her dad had said to her recently, the words didn't offer comfort. Though she still heard his voice in her head, she no longer confused it with God. Though her loss of faith had hurt her father, she couldn't pretend to believe.

These days she related most to Job's trials. Like the biblical figure, Rachel was sure there could be no purpose to all she had endured over the last several years—the death of her husband when an aneurysm had burst in his abdomen, the betrayal by her best friend, the loss of her business. Unlike Job, she thought of fleeing, though she had no idea where she would go or whether she would be able to make things better for her children.

"As with Job," her father had told her, "all this is a test of faith."

"Is that the category for your visits to Angela? A test?"

He'd looked genuinely shocked. "Of course not. She's in need of my care, of spiritual guidance."

"Even though she betrayed me?"

"Especially because of that." And, as he'd said a thousand times before, he had told her, "My ministry to another doesn't lessen my love for you."

"Your visits to her feel like another betrayal," Rachel had confessed angrily.

He'd looked at her sternly, then, in the way that had always, always made her obey him. "You know better than that. Prayer and study will show you that that is as ridiculous as your assertion that God has abandoned you. I'm so disappointed in you."

Like the Look, his "I'm so disappointed" speech usually guaranteed she'd strive to please him even as the phrase cut her to the quick. But for the first time in her life, she had retreated, feeling lost and confused and emotionally abandoned. Now she no longer called her father except to make arrangements for her children to visit him.

She felt as though the support, understanding and compassion she wanted for herself had been given away to others, especially Angela. And, her dad seemed to believe she was asking him to choose between his ministry and her. Yet she had simply wanted some of his boundless compassion for herself. Maybe the wanting made her selfish, but she hadn't been able to banish it.

Seven blocks from her home, she drove past the brick-front building that had housed Victorian Rose Antiques. The green awning shaded the front window, which still posted the sign that the business had been closed by the DEA. Since their merchandise was tainted by the drug trade, it had been seized. The day Angela had been arraigned, the bank had called in the loan that had secured the purchase of all that merchandise.

And now it was all *her* problem.

Rachel's daily refrain echoed in her head. *What in the world had Angela been thinking?* Even Angela herself hadn't been able to answer. All Rachel knew was that Angela had plea-bargained the charges against her and provided the names that had led Agent Micah McLeod to the bigger fish he had really been after.

But was that bigger fish now after *her?*

Rachel's hands grew clammy with the memory of the rock shattering the window and bringing her out of a restless sleep. Since she no longer had the e-mail or the letter with their simple, one-line demands—I want my $500,000—the police had no reason to think the rock was anything more than a prank. She had told them about the notes, immediately knowing how lame her story sounded.

"Call us," the investigating officer had told her, "if another note comes." A month had passed since then, and until Micah McLeod had showed up yesterday afternoon, she had hoped the police were right about the rock and notes being a prank.

The fear was back, and she hated it.

Think about today, she told herself. Today would be

a good day because of the appointment she had after work. Jane Clark, one of her best—and wealthiest—clients from the antique shop, had a referral for Rachel. The whispered promise of returning to the work that she loved sang through her. Today, she reminded herself, was a new day.

After a half-hour on the road, Rachel parked her car behind one of the hotels that lined I-70. She went through the service entrance, clocked in and went to work for the first of her three jobs—this one as a maid.

She was so used to being invisible that she didn't even look twice when a man came out of one of the rooms and approached her. His steps slowed, and she looked up.

Micah McLeod, his dark-brown eyes steady on her.

Her heart gave a familiar lurch—it always did when she saw him. She didn't want to notice that he looked good, but he did. He wore jeans, a Western-style shirt, cowboy boots and a Stetson with the ease of a man who had grown up in the clothes rather than adopting them like some packaged country-music singer. She knew under his hat was a full head of hair, the dark strands liberally streaked with gray.

She forced herself to look away and wished he would walk right past her, somehow knowing that he wouldn't. He came to a halt next to her cart, blocking her way back into the room she was cleaning.

"What in the world are you doing here?" he asked.

"Working." She stuffed the linens she had just stripped off a bed into the hamper at the bottom of the cart.

"Working," he repeated. "Why?"

A sharp retort was at the tip of her tongue when she noticed one of the hotel managers at the end of the hall. Jason Laird, a young man fresh out of college. His pretentious attitude grated more often than not, and he had made it clear maids were to be seen and not heard.

"For the usual reasons," she said managing to keep annoyance out of her voice as Jason came closer. "Is there something you need?"

"Not anything you can give me here." Micah turned around to see who she was watching.

"Good morning, sir," Jason said to Micah. "Is everything okay?"

"Fine," he responded.

"Enjoy your stay." Jason raised an eyebrow at her and cocked his head toward the room she was cleaning, his unspoken message as clear as a command. *Get back to work.*

Rachel pulled clean sheets from her cart while Micah stood there watching her as though she were some exotic species he was studying in a zoo. "If you'll excuse me," she said as she brushed past him.

He followed her into the room. "If you're going to work in a hotel, why not turn your house into a bed-and-breakfast like you once talked about?"

The suggestion frayed her temper. How could he know so much about her hopes and dreams when she had clearly known nothing about his? Once he had told her about a ranch in Wyoming, his description of a home so vivid she had imagined living there. Like everything else last spring, that had most likely been a lie, too.

She snapped a clean sheet open and it floated across the mattress. Efficiently, she tucked the sheet around the mattress and did her best to ignore Micah's large presence.

He simply stood there, waiting with the patience that was so much a part of him. She finished making the bed and did a visual scan of the room to make sure she hadn't missed anything. All that was left was to vacuum.

When she retrieved the vacuum cleaner from the hallway, he blocked her way back into the room.

"Rachel, talk to me. Why are you working here?"

"Because I need the job."

He moved to the side so she could enter the room, then followed her. "This is the best job you could get?"

Mentally counting to ten, she plugged in the vacuum. "There's nothing wrong with this job."

"Okay, maybe that was out of line, but you're the most capable person I know. I've never known anyone smarter than you. You could have gone back into banking or—"

"So why would I stoop so low?" she interrupted, turning around to face him, last spring's events so much at the surface she trembled. "Have you ever stuck around after your investigations are concluded to see what happened next? Or is it just on to your next assignment with your carefully taken notes so when you get called back to testify you remember the...how did you put it? Oh, yes...the pertinent facts of the case."

He took off his hat and thumbed the brim before looking at her. "I remember everything, Rachel. And I regret—"

"Regret doesn't feed my children," she said, the last tenuous thread on her temper shredding. "And as for going back to work at the bank, nobody would hire me to be a teller, much less a financial analyst—not after learning my business partner had been convicted of money-laundering."

"That was Angela London, not you."

"And weren't you the man who once told me that the quality of a man's character can be measured in the friends he has?"

"I'm sorry."

"No doubt." She looked up then, and met his gaze. "Go away, Micah McLeod. If I never see you or talk to you or—" She swallowed the lump in her throat and willed the tears burning her eyes to go away.

"What's going on?" Jason Laird stood in the doorway.

"Nothing," Micah said. "I'm leaving." He slipped past Jason who watched with his arms folded over his chest.

"You come with me," Jason said to Rachel. "Right now."

She knew what was coming, but like so much else over the last few months, being chewed out for talking to a guest was one more thing to be endured.

"Your services are no longer needed," Jason said as soon as he sat himself down behind his desk.

"You're firing me?" She had expected to be bawled out—not dismissed.

"You know the rules about contact with guests," he said, "and your behavior toward our guest just now is completely unacceptable."

Locking her jaw so her chin wouldn't tremble, Rachel stared at a point beyond Jason's shoulder while he finished dressing her down. Fifteen minutes later she clocked out and left the motel. It wasn't yet 9:00 a.m.

She got in her car and sat there a moment, feeling her debts weighing her down and the empty light on the fuel gauge taunting her with this latest failure.

She needed the money from this job, meager as it was. She couldn't go home. Be bold as a lion, she told herself, gazing down the road where another dozen motels lined the street. She hated the idea of another maid's job, but it was routine work that fit with the schedule for her other jobs. *Bold as a lion* would be to march down to the bank and apply for her old job in the trust department.

But today she was only bold as a hungry kitten so, irritated with her own lack of temerity, she headed for a motel a block away where she filled out her first application. Once more the anonymous demand for the half-million dollars flitted through her head, this time making her laugh silently. Like she would be looking for a sustenance job if she had access to that kind of money.

Even with the promise of better money that would likely come as a result of her appointment with Jane Clark, any income would be weeks to months in coming. Which made today simply another one to survive.

By the time she filled out her ninth application, any humor she had seen in her situation had long since vanished.

* * *

"Hello, Tommy," Micah said to Angela London's old boyfriend, surprised he had found the man the first place he looked—an upscale pool hall a couple of blocks from the historic Colorado Hotel. The clientele this early in the day was thin—Tommy Manderoll was playing alone. Waiting to score a sale, Micah was sure, since he was the one who had introduced Angela to drugs and the promise of easy money.

The man was nice-looking enough that Micah understood why Angela had gotten involved with him. But he was a user through and through.

Tommy didn't look up until he had taken his shot, neatly pocketing a ball in the side hole. His eyes narrowed when he recognized Micah. "I don't have anything to say to you."

Micah shrugged and held out his hands in a placating gesture. "I haven't asked you anything."

"Yet." Tommy moved around the table, chalking up the end of his cue as he went. "Whatever you're selling, I'm not buying." He hit another ball, this time missing. Scowling at Micah, he accused, "You've been following me."

"I just got to town," Micah said, leaning against an adjoining table and crossing his ankles as though he had the whole day. "You have some reason to think you're being followed?"

Tommy snorted. "Like I'd tell you."

"I dunno," Micah said crossing his arms. "A man paranoid enough to think I'm following him probably has something to hide."

"I'm an open book. Ask my probation officer."

One thing the man had proven last spring was his knack for self-preservation. He'd provided the DA the final pieces of evidence that had convicted Angela, all for the price of his freedom, of course. The man had copped a misdemeanor plea and had been given probation and community service. And Micah knew as sure as he was standing here that Tommy was still dealing and equally certain that if he searched the man or his car, he wouldn't find anything but chewing gum in his pockets or his car.

"Have you seen Simon Graden lately?" Graden had been the big fish that got away last spring without so much as an indictment touching him. Though Graden hadn't been charged, it was only a matter of time, since too many paths of money trickled toward his door. Even if Angela hadn't told him that Graden had threatened her a week before she was sentenced, he would have been Micah's first suspect.

Tommy took longer lining up the next shot, and once more he missed pocketing the ball. "We don't exactly run in the same circles."

Micah knew that to be true. Upscale as this place might be, it lacked the five-star amenities that Graden would expect.

The man was quite wealthy—to most people he was merely one of Aspen's millionaires. Unlike most others involved with the drug trade at his level, the man had no discernable organization. In spite of all the smoke and mirrors he hid behind, Micah was sure they would soon get him.

Since Tommy had turned on Angela for a price, he figured the man was capable of doing the same to Rachel. "There's a rumor he's looking for a missing half-million dollars. You wouldn't know anything about that?"

"Nope," Tommy instantly said without looking at Micah.

Micah didn't believe him. "And you wouldn't know why he thinks Rachel Neesham has it."

Tommy jerked his head up, his gaze colliding with Micah's. So that had surprised him. Interesting.

"Miss Goody Goody?" Tommy shook his head. "That boggles the mind."

"I don't hear you denying anything."

Once more Tommy shook his head. "The only rumor I've heard about Rachel Neesham is she's in debt up to her eyeballs and that she'll probably lose her house."

That news kicked Micah hard. He supposed he should have seen that coming, but he hadn't. Just like he hadn't imagined her working as a maid in a hotel.

"What about Two-bits Perez?" Micah asked. Two-bits had been a paid snitch and a good "friend" of Tommy's.

Tommy took his time lining up another shot, his hand steady as a rock when he hit it. "Haven't seen him since last spring."

"Even though you're buddies."

Tommy shook his head. "He's no friend of mine."

If the friendship had dissolved, it could be for a lot of reasons, Micah thought. Tommy could have found out Two-bits was a snitch. Or Tommy could have stopped supplying Two-bits with his drugs. Since Micah had a few questions to ask the man, he hoped the informant was healthy and easy to track down.

Micah pulled a business card out of his pocket and handed it to Tommy. "If you hear anything I might want to know, you'll call me?"

"What's it gonna pay?"

Micah gave the young criminal a threatening smile. "The opportunity to keep living as a free man."

THREE

"I was about to give up on you," Jane Clark said after Rachel rang her doorbell a few minutes after six that same evening. "I tried calling your old cell phone number, but it's been disconnected."

"Yes, it has," Rachel said. The cell phone, no matter how convenient, was one of the luxuries she could no longer afford.

Jane's house was on the outskirts of Aspen, an hour's drive from the job she had finally secured on the thirteenth application she had filled out. She'd had just enough time to change out of her new maid's uniform and into a simple skirt and sweater before embarking on the drive.

"No matter," Jane said, smiling over her shoulder. "You're here now."

Rachel followed Jane through a huge foyer and down a ten-foot-wide hallway that led toward the library. Last year, Rachel had been here numerous times while antique walnut paneling from a chateau in Reims was being installed in the library.

Jane had a love for the finest in European antiques, from paintings and statuary to exquisite stained glass and architectural elements. Then Rachel hadn't minded the long drive because having clients in Aspen meant Victorian Rose Antiques had made it to the big leagues.

Jane ushered Rachel into the library. The room looked even more stunning than she remembered. The wood gleamed and hidden lights expertly showcased Jane's collection of Italian urns. This room represented nineteenth-century carpentry at its finest. Caught up in the details, Rachel didn't notice the man standing near the French limestone mantel until he cleared his throat.

"This is my friend, Simon Graden," Jane said, taking Rachel by the elbow and drawing her forward. "When he told me that he was looking for architectural pieces for his home, I told him you were the person he needed to talk to."

The name was familiar, though Rachel couldn't place from where.

"Your reputation precedes you," he said, moving toward her and holding out his hand.

Something in his tone was off somehow, making her shiver.

After the perfunctory handshake, Rachel asked, "What are you looking for, Mr. Graden?"

"It's true then. You still are in business?"

"I no longer have a store, if that's what you're asking." If the man had been anywhere in Colorado over the summer, he would have read about the scandal-related demise of Victorian Rose Antiques in just about any newspaper.

"But you can get me merchandise?"

"Only the best to be had," Jane assured him, while Rachel said, "The purchase of antiques requires patience if you're looking for a particular piece."

Jane chuckled and moved toward the door. "Something I know from firsthand experience." She motioned toward Rachel. "You'll join us for dinner, of course."

"I'm afraid not. I've—"

"Got those darling children to get home to."

"Yes."

"Then I need to tell the cook we'll only be two for dinner. Sure you won't change your mind?" When Rachel shook her head, Jane said, "Simon, I've made the introduction, and I'm leaving you in very good hands. Rachel, help yourself to a beverage." Another wave, this time toward the built-in bar.

Rachel watched the door close behind Jane, not at all sure what to make of Simon Graden. He acted as though he was fifty, but, despite his gray hair, he looked young enough to be in his early thirties. Wanting to give her hands something to do besides flutter nervously, she opened the small refrigerator and took out a bottle of water.

"You still haven't told me what you're looking for," she said, twisting off the cap and taking a sip.

"A half-million dollars worth of merchandise," he said evenly.

That again. Her first temptation was to say something flip, like, There's a lot of that going around. Her second, more concrete thought was that she must not have heard him correctly. "I'm sorry, Mr. Graden. I don't think I quite understand. Are you planning to go into the antiques business?"

"I have a business." He smiled, almost gently, and she caught a glint of steel in his blue eyes. "And it's missing a half-million dollars."

She felt the blood drain from her face. Surely he wasn't talking about the anonymous e-mail and the letter demanding money. She took another a sip of water, then shivered as the cold liquid trickled down her throat. His voice startled her when he broke the silence.

"Does that sum mean something to you?"

This was no dark alley where danger lurked, but she was at once as terrified as she might have been facing an armed mugger.

"Business transactions should be simple, don't you think?" He shook his head, crossed the room back to the mantel where he had left a goblet, which he picked up, then smoothed a finger across one of the facets of cut glass. "An exchange of money for goods or services rendered."

Rachel swiped a sweaty palm across her forehead, wishing her brain would engage sometime soon and that the panic in her chest would subside. This was bizarre beyond words. This meeting was supposed to lead to good things, to renew a career she had loved. It wasn't supposed to be one more fear to pile on all the others.

"Reliable resources tell me that you have—or can get—what I want."

"Antiques?"

He clucked his tongue. "Rachel, I've been told you're a smart woman." He looked steadily at her, those blue eyes cold and clear, "I've been told you already have the…" He paused. "…The item I want."

Rachel felt completely disconnected, hating how much this all made perfect sense and how nothing about this situation was the least bit sensible. How would Jane know someone like this man—someone shaking her down like the third-grade bully who had regularly taken her lunch money.

Only much more dangerous.

"You don't have to look so stunned, Rachel. You understand my requirements, don't you?"

The simple answer was yes. But she couldn't bring herself to say the word, somehow sure that doing so would mean admitting that she had a half-million dollars that she'd never even seen.

The man had said something about goods or services. "What services?"

"A refund," he corrected. "That should have been returned months ago."

"A refund?" Muzzy from the conflicting thoughts going through her head, she looked toward the door where Jane had disappeared.

He smiled. "I knew you'd understand."

Rachel lifted a hand toward the door. "Jane thinks you want my expertise in antiques."

"It's best if it remains that way, as I'm sure you'll agree."

"But—"

"Now, then. When can I expect delivery?"

"I don't have your—"

"Then I suggest you talk to whomever does."

The library door clicked open on the heels of a quick knock, and Jane breezed into the room. "Cook says dinner is ready whenever we are. Is Rachel going to be able to help you?"

"I'm sure of it," he said with a smile, handing Rachel a picture that had somehow magically appeared in his hand. "She was just telling me about her family."

But she hadn't been. Numb and feeling completely out of her depth, Rachel glanced down at the photograph. It was of her father, Sarah and Andy at the park a couple of blocks from her house. Andy had the Blue's Clues Band-Aid on his knee from where he had skinned it.

The day before.

This picture had been taken yesterday.

"You have a lovely family," he said. "I can see why you're so proud of little…Sarah, did you say her name was? And Andy. He looks like a wild one."

This man knows the names of my children. He has a picture of my children. She stared at the photograph, looking for all the world like one she might have taken. Only she hadn't.

"He's four now, isn't he, Rachel?" Jane asked.

"Yes." Rachel looked up, found Simon Graden standing close enough to touch, a benevolent-looking smile on his face. Then she looked into his eyes and found them to be as cold as the fear slithering through her belly.

"There's nothing more compelling than family, is there? So nice your father can spend time with your children in the park. And he's a retired minister, you say?"

Once more, Rachel nodded, her neck and lips stiff. This man was threatening her. And if he could get close enough to take pictures, he could get close enough to do worse.

He extended his hand again, this time with a business card between his fingers. "You'll call me as soon as you can arrange delivery?"

Rachel automatically took the card, a slight nod to her head, the gesture rooted in the fear swamping her.

"Oh, this is great," Jane said, crossing the room, a wide smile lighting her face, and giving Rachel a squeeze. "I've been so worried about you with that whole nasty business with Angela. And I just knew that you'd be able to get back in business again if you had a little help. It's no wonder you're looking a little dazed. Sometimes good news is almost harder to take in than bad news."

Rachel glanced from Simon to Jane, both of them smiling as though things were wonderful and she wasn't teetering at the edge of an emotional cliff. She swallowed the bile that burned the back of her throat.

"You should thank Jane," Simon said. "Friends who will go out of their way for you are rare."

"Yes," Rachel agreed faintly, looking around for her purse. All she wanted to do was leave. Run. Gather up her children and her father and simply disappear.

"After you've had a chance to research that one item you were going to check on when you get home," Simon said, "you can call me."

Rachel looked from him to Jane, who smiled.

"Now that I know you're back in business again, we'll talk. I'm remodeling the patio and I was thinking a big bronze urn would be just thing. You know, like that Roman one you showed me last year." As if realizing she was about to go off on a tangent, Jane laughed. "I'll save that for next time. It's so nice to see you again, Rachel."

"You, too." Good manners made Rachel respond as she went out the door. Somehow she kept from running down the wide marble hallway to the front entry. Outside, the setting sun was lodged between two peaks, streaming golden rays across the valley. She stared unseeingly at the beauty for a moment, her mind utterly blank, then ran down the wide flagstone steps toward her car.

He wanted her to call him. But she didn't have his money, didn't have any idea how to convince him that she didn't.

In her car, she jammed her key into the ignition and noticed her hand shaking. As the engine revved, she looked at the crumpled picture of her family. Tears burning her eyes, she smoothed out the glossy paper, her fingers lingering over the images of her son and her daughter.

He knew how to find them. And he had threatened her, all the while making it sound as though she was agreeing to find some rare antique for him. What could she even say to anyone else? He'd made it look as though the photograph was hers. He hadn't said, "I'll hurt your children."

He didn't have to.

She put the car into gear and headed down the picturesque road that led back to the highway and her hour-long drive home. She glanced at the fuel gauge, praying she had enough gas to make it home, while sweat coated her palms.

She'd hoped for a reprieve. Instead, this was one more disaster, and this one scared her like nothing else. She had no idea what to do.

Call Micah McLeod.

That would happen right after manna fell from heaven.

Still, the thought haunted her throughout the ride and didn't go away after she picked up Sarah and Andy from her next-door neighbor's house or after she put them to bed. It stayed right with her as she went through her evening chores, making and discarding a dozen different plans. Eventually, she found herself staring blindly out the kitchen window, her reflection taunting her.

A sound outside in the darkness startled her, and she stepped to the side and peered into the night. One more thing she was afraid of, one more fear to conquer since that rock had been thrown through her front door.

A rap on the back door a few feet away made her jump.

"Rachel, it's Micah."

She recognized his voice, and slowly moved to the door, unwilling to send him away, unwilling to invite him in.

"Rachel?"

She suspected that he saw her, or at least her shadow, but still she hesitated. How could she open the door to this man who had told her one lie after another, all in the name of doing his job?

"Rachel, please. Let's just talk."

She switched on the outside light, and there he stood

on the back porch, looking tall and dependable, like a man she could lean on if she had a problem.

In her dreams.

"I'm sorry you got fired this morning."

"Nothing travels faster than bad news." The fact she had almost forgotten about that surprised her. Of course, that was no longer the worst thing that had happened today.

He stared at her through the screen door, holding his Stetson in front of him like a shield. With a sigh, she unlatched the door. "Come in."

He slipped past her, and though she wanted to be angry at him for his past actions, at the moment, all that was insignificant. Annoyed with the feelings feathering through her chest—like relief…hope—she watched him, wishing this man had truly been the friend he had once seemed to be. But she knew better than anyone how futile wishes were.

She went to the refrigerator and retrieved a pitcher of iced tea. "Tell me why you really came back."

He looked at her sharply, then away, as though deciding what he should say.

"You always do that." With more force than necessary, she clunked several ice cubes into one glass, then another. "Thinking. Weighing. It's like you're trying to remember which lie you told and how to tell another without getting caught."

"I suppose that's how it must seem to you," he said, setting his hat on the table.

"Lies by omission," she said, "are still lies. No evasions this time, Micah. Why did you come back?

And don't tell me it was to apologize. The time for that was months ago." Despite her best intentions to be unemotional, her voice caught when she added, "I might have forgiven you then."

"I *am* sorry." He took a step toward her, then abruptly stopped when she held up her palm. "And you do deserve the truth, all of it." He raked an impatient hand through his hair. "It's just that the truth is never quite as black and white as it should be."

"You mean like Angela going to prison and her drug-dealing boyfriend getting off scot-free."

Micah nodded. "And like you getting caught in someone else's mess. I'm sorry for that, Rachel. All of it." This time, he tucked his fingers into the top of his jeans pockets and faced her square on, his chin lifted, as though he was facing a firing squad. "Most of all, I'm sorry for lying to you."

She held a glass filled with tea. "And that's why you came back."

His gaze at once skittered away from hers.

That simple thing ignited her temper all over again, and she slammed her glass onto the counter. "Get out." She marched across the kitchen and picked up his hat, the felt absurdly soft against her fingertips. "Take your hat and go. I can't believe I'm stupid enough to be glad you came here tonight. What in the world was I thinking? I'm not going to put up with you pondering every single thing you say because whatever comes out of your mouth will be a lie. And if its not a lie, it certainly won't be the truth."

For an instant, she caught his gaze, then looked away.

The months of frustration continued to pour out of her. "It's been the worst day ever. Somebody threatened me and my kids tonight, and then there you are at my door and I think, great. The hero in the white hat has finally shown up." She thrust his taupe-colored hat into his hands. "Well, wrong again."

Hating her burst of temper, she held open the back door and motioned for him to leave. He stood in the middle of the kitchen, though, planted as solidly as the old pine tree in the middle of the yard.

"What do you mean, someone threatened you tonight?" he asked, the question cutting to the heart of the fear swamping her.

"It doesn't concern you." She pushed a strand of hair behind her ear.

"Does this have anything to do with the money?"

"Why would you think that?"

"Angela called me after you came to visit her," Micah said. "She was worried about you." He paused, and when Rachel's jaw tightened, he said, "Because she thinks she knows who might be behind the threat."

"She told me she didn't know." Rachel dropped her head, pinching the bridge of her nose. "She lied again."

"To protect you."

"And how does not telling me protect me?" she asked, her temper again at the surface. "More importantly, how does it protect my kids?" She plunged a hand into the pocket of her long swirling skirt, and withdrew a crumpled photograph that she held out to him. "My family is everything to me."

"I know that." Micah looked from her to the images

on the picture. Her father. Andy. Sarah. All of them unaware they had been photographed. "You didn't take this picture?"

She shook her head.

"Who gave this to you?" His intuition told him that this was a huge breakthrough, and as a DEA agent he felt the thrill of the chase. But as the man who loved Rachel, he wanted her to deny it all the same, hating the idea of Rachel in danger, hating that she might have come face-to-face with the ultimate villain.

"First tell me what you know."

He took a step toward her. "This isn't a game, Rachel."

Her mouth tightened, and for a moment he didn't think she would tell him

She held his eyes in a challenge. "Simon Graden."

He wished she hadn't just confirmed his suspicion— and his worst fear.

FOUR

Micah didn't even pretend not to know who Rachel meant. The man—the kingpin—he had been after last spring. The one who was still in business while Rachel had paid too big a price for being a suspect.

Her eyes were on him, direct and clear and demanding the truth. Facts, he could give her. The truth was a lot harder. "Tell me what happened."

"He threatened me." She shook the crumpled photograph. "Worse, he threatened my children. And the scariest part is, it was all so polite. Courteous. He could repeat every single thing he said to me from a pulpit and the meaning would seem innocent to anyone else."

She shivered again, this time reaching for the sweater she'd left hanging over the back of a chair. Nerves, Micah knew, because his own were stretched thin. At the moment, he didn't care about the investigation or the instructions from his superior that Graden be taken down. Micah wanted Rachel and her children far from this situation before anything could happen.

"Start from the beginning, Rachel." Inwardly, he

winced, knowing he sounded just like a detached investigator.

And she did, telling him about the call from Jane Clark and how excited she'd been, because for the first time since last spring, she hoped there might be a way out of the pit she was in. How frightened she had been at Graden's benign-sounding threat. How recently this picture had been taken, and how close to home. How she wanted simply to disappear along with her children and her father.

"That part is a good idea," Micah said, gesturing toward the phone. "Pick up the phone, call your dad, and I can have you on the road before midnight."

Her expression crumpled even more as her glance strayed to the clock on the stove where the time read that it was a few minutes before ten.

"Rachel?" He wanted to gather her close and stand between her and whatever was hurting her so. He didn't know how things could get worse, but he was certain they were about to.

She shook her head. "It's too late."

"What are you talking about?" he asked. For her to be reluctant to call her dad, no matter how late, didn't make a bit of sense.

She lifted her chin and looked at him, sighing. "The truth is that my dad and I aren't talking right now."

Her completely neutral tone didn't jibe with the tension radiating from her body as she once again wrapped her arms around herself. Micah was dead sure she had no idea how much she revealed with that protective gesture.

"Are you going to tell me why, or do we get to play twenty questions about this, too?" he asked, sitting down at the kitchen table. He took a sip of tea from his glass.

She turned away from him, but not before he saw a private, hopeful smile dissolve into near tears. A memory manacled him to the chair like a prisoner, and he wondered if she had been grabbed by the same one.

He had been working for her for only a few days when the handyman, Smitty Jones, had dropped a heavy armoire on Micah's foot. Rachel hadn't believed his assertion that his injury was nothing more than a bruise and she'd demanded he show her. After he'd put his boot back on, she somehow ended up inviting him to dinner. He wondered now if the invitation had surprised her as much as it had him.

He'd come, sure that he'd find the missing pieces of evidence he needed to prove that she was involved in selling drugs and laundering money. Instead, he'd practiced T-ball with Sarah and built a Lego fort with Andy. Instead, he had cooked dinner side by side with Rachel because it was an excuse to get close to her. And he'd forgotten about the investigation for a few cherished hours. He'd nearly kissed her that night, and as he watched her now, he regretted that he hadn't, regretted that he'd never have another chance.

He'd been welcome then, trusted then.

Abruptly, he folded his legs under the chair, the present coming back into focus.

"You might as well tell me what's going on between you and your dad," Micah said. "You know I'm going to find out anyway."

Her eyes strayed to the calendar, held to the refrigerator by a couple of magnets. "It wouldn't do any good to call him tonight, anyway. He won't be there."

"Because," Micah prompted.

Her lips tightened as she glanced at him, then looked away, pacing around the spacious kitchen as she wiped an invisible speck on the counter and moved a canister into position. "Because he goes to see Angela every other week, and he left this morning. He won't be back until tomorrow evening."

"Is that the reason you two aren't talking?" Micah could imagine how that would rankle—having her father remain loyal to the woman who had betrayed her.

"One of several." She gave her attention to another microscopic speck on the counter.

Micah glanced at the photograph she had left on the table. "But your kids see him."

"Of course. He's family."

"And this is a life-or-death situation, potentially."

"Thanks for the reassurance."

Micah stood. "You wanted the truth, Rachel. So whatever your issues with your dad—"

"I'll handle it," she said, her tone flat.

"Okay." Since she was already annoyed, he decided to broach the next sensitive subject. "Until I can get your family to safety, you need to have someone here with you."

She shook her head.

"This isn't like last spring," he said, "when you were suspected of being one of the bad guys. Your safety is paramount. Think about it. Graden keeps raising the stakes, by your own admission. First an e-mail, then an anonymous letter, then a rock through your window and now today's threat. Keeping you, Sarah and Andy out of harm's way is just as important to me as—"

"Getting your man?"

The accusation carrying the sting of truth, Micah came to a stop in front of her. "Seeing you reconciled with your dad," he corrected, taking the washcloth from her and tossing it in the sink. "Seeing you have your dreams for this house come true."

Her lovely eyes clouded even more, making Micah feel like a heel for having brought that up, remembering how last spring she had begun the application process to create a bed-and-breakfast out of this stately old house.

"Another pipe dream," she whispered.

"If keeping the house is an issue," he said, reaching for her hand, "I'll give you the money." He hadn't intended to say that.

"Give?" She stepped away from him. "You or the DEA?"

"This has nothing to do with the investigation."

"That's taking guilt a little far, don't you think? Even for you?"

"Lend, then." *Guilt.* She had that nailed. Guilt or not, he'd gladly give her the money. If it chased the shadows from her eyes, it would be worth every cent. "Until you're back on your feet."

"No."

She looked at him then, and once more he found himself drawing comparisons to last spring. Then, her eyes had been filled with delight and contentment. She'd loved her work, her children and the life she had created for herself after her husband had died. Micah didn't like knowing he was responsible for taking that away. She swallowed, and his gaze was drawn to her pulse fluttering at the base of her neck.

"If you're back here to pull the rug from under me like you did last spring…" Her gaze searched his while she paused, then she continued in a whisper. "…That would just about kill me."

Needing to touch her and hoping she wouldn't slap his hand away, he brushed a tendril of her fine hair away from her face. "I'm here to help you, Rachel. I promise."

"But you still have to get your man."

"Yes, I do." His hand trembled when he let it drop to his side. Relief she had allowed that much? Fear that he wanted more? He didn't know.

Rachel held his gaze for a long silent moment, grateful that he hadn't looked away as he so often did. The depths of his dark-brown eyes seemed kind and compassionate to her, but then, they had last spring, too. She wanted to trust what he was saying. Oh, how she wanted it. But, with the memories came that ever-present fear.

Suddenly aware of how close he was and too tempted to lean into his comforting strength, she stepped away. "I'll talk to my dad when he gets home."

"Good."

"I'm not that keen about taking the kids out of school," she said. "They'll fall behind."

"Are you saying that you'll agree to go into a safe house?" he asked, leaning against the kitchen counter and looking as though he belonged here. She remembered thinking so last spring. She'd been a fool then. She could only hope she wasn't now.

As the memory of Graden's threats surfaced again, she closed her eyes. Micah hadn't questioned any of that being real, and that was something, at least. It was the first time anyone had taken her seriously in a while. Finally she nodded.

"Good," he said, once more. "Now about having someone keep an eye on you—"

"We'll cross that bridge tomorrow. Since all this happened just this afternoon, Mr. Graden can't expect that I'll deliver tonight."

"If I were him," Micah said, "I'd be expecting you to run."

"Where would I go?"

"People who run don't need a place to go—merely something to run from."

As unsettling as the suggestion was—especially since she'd had that very thought—Rachel shook her head. "He's not going to do anything tonight."

"I'll stay." He waited until she looked at him. "Keep a watch out. Allow you to get a full night's sleep and maybe erase those circles under your eyes."

"No." *She had circles under her eyes?* Disconcerted that she wanted to look good for him, she looked away from his penetrating gaze. With effort, she brought her thoughts back to the topic at hand. Him staying and watching over her and her children. She decided that she had lost her mind since she was far too tempted to take him up on his offer. Too tempted to trust him. Under the circumstances, that was stupid. "We'll be fine tonight."

Micah couldn't blame her for refusing the offer. She had no reason to trust him. He picked up his glass and took a healthy swallow of tea while she watched him, the silence between them just as tense as their conversation had been.

"What's your schedule tomorrow?" he asked.

"I've got to be at the motel before six-thirty," she said with a slight shake to her head. "I'd forgotten all about that. Tomorrow is my first full day on the new job. Six-thirty to two-thirty."

"And the kids, what do they do until school starts?"

"Dolly Jackson comes over. She's a sixteen-year-old who lives two doors down. She walks them to school and my dad picks up Andy when kindergarten lets out at noon, except for the days when he's gone."

"Like tomorrow?"

"Then Andy goes home with Jeremy Simpson and I pick him up after I get off work." Rachel was back to her nervous cleaning while she talked. "I guess I should talk to their teachers—let them know the kids will be out of school for a while."

Micah was glad to hear the kids were still friendly with some of their classmates, since it was clear that Rachel had been shunned by many of her supposed friends.

"I'd rather you didn't. That would immediately telegraph to Graden that you're not going to cooperate.

Tomorrow, you need to go through your day just as normal, and when the kids get out of school tomorrow afternoon, I'll have things set up." When she didn't look at him or respond, he tacked on, "Okay?"

"Okay," she agreed with a quick nod.

Micah drained the last of the tea, put on his hat, and headed for the back door. "I'll see you tomorrow, then."

He went outside and paused at the bottom of the stoop, letting his eyes adjust to the darkness of the backyard, waiting for her to close and lock the door behind him.

"Micah," she called from inside the screen.

"Yeah." He turned around and drank in the sight of her framed by the light above the kitchen table.

"This isn't going to get all fouled up like the last investigation, is it?"

Making sure that he was looking straight at her, he said, "I'll do my best to make sure that it doesn't." He took off his hat and cleared his throat. "I hate what happened to you, Rachel, and if I had it to do over— I'd do a lot of things different this time."

She stared at him a long moment before murmuring goodnight and closing the door. He stood motionless until he heard the click of the lock, then headed around the side yard. Deep within the shadow of the big blue spruce between her house and her neighbor's, he came to a stop, studying the street as far as he could see in both directions. Only a couple of parked cars on the block and they looked empty. No telltale movements or shifting of shadows that indicated Rachel's house was being watched.

Only then did he head for his car where he began making the calls that would ensure Rachel's safety.

The next day was the longest ever for Rachel. Her imagination galloped in a dozen different directions. Though Micah had been at the house when she left for work, assuring her that he'd keep an eye on the kids as they went through their day, she worried. And she kept worrying until she picked Andy up from the Simpsons' house, following the normal routine. Despite Micah's promise to watch over them, if he was anywhere around, she didn't see him.

"Jeremy got a basketball hoop for his birthday," Andy told her the minute his seatbelt was fastened, and they were on their way. "I think we need one. We could put it on the side of the driveway next to the garage."

"Need, huh?" They'd had the talk several times about the difference between need and want. She had promised both of the kids they would have everything they needed, but for a while they might not have the things they wanted.

When she looked at him through the rearview mirror, he grinned. "It's real cool, Mom, but I guess I don't *need* one."

"Tell me about your day at school."

"We did all kinds of stuff and then Cindy Mac-Allister threw up and there was a great big mess and, boy, did it stink. Mrs. Wells said that's 'cause of bacteria. Did you know that, Mom?"

"I'd heard that." Rachel turned onto their street, her breath catching when she realized the car that had been behind them turned onto the quiet street also. "What else did you do?"

"I don't remember."

His not remembering was the usual, and Rachel knew that his day would come out in bits and pieces between now and bedtime.

The Jeep Wrangler that Micah had been driving when he came to the door this morning was in front of her house, the sight familiar, somehow, and reassuring. As always, the doubts immediately surfaced, despite Micah's looking her straight in the eye, everything about him proclaiming he'd told her the truth.

She'd thought about their conversation for a good part of her sleepless night, eventually deciding he had no reason to lie this time, no reason to be here except for the one he'd told her. Maybe her dad was right. Maybe the first step was to begin trusting again.

She turned into the driveway and pressed the garage opener. Through the open side door, Rachel saw a woman about her own age sitting at the picnic table talking on a cell phone. When she saw Rachel, she waved and stood up.

"Mom, there's a stranger in our backyard," Andy announced.

"Yes, there is." Rachel unfastened her seatbelt and looked back at her son. "Why don't you sit here for a minute while I find out what she wants."

"Aw, Mom. I need to get a snack." He fumbled at his own seatbelt. "*Need*, Mom. I'm starving."

"Just give me a minute." By the time she got out of the car, the woman was halfway across the lawn, a welcoming smile on her face. Not smiling back was impossible.

"I'm Erin Asher," she said, pulling a wallet from her pocket and extending it to Rachel. "Micah sent me ahead. In fact, he's right behind you."

Rachel glanced at the official-looking badge and identification for the DEA before looking toward the street. Micah was getting out of the car that had followed her with another man. The reinforcements Micah had promised had arrived.

For once he'd told her the truth.

The constriction in her chest eased, and she said to Andy, "You can get out of the car now."

"I bet you didn't expect to find a stranger in your backyard when you came home." Erin shook hands with Andy after he came around the car. "You must be Andy."

"Andrew Chester Neesham," he said, shaking her hand briskly, "I'm named after my grandfathers."

"Are you? Now that's something."

Just then, Andy caught sight of Micah around the side of the house, and a huge smile lit his face as he ran toward the man. "Sarah said you came back." He launched himself into Micah's arms. "I'm really glad to see you."

"Me, too, buddy." Micah met Rachel's gaze over the top of her son's head before looking back at the boy. "You've grown a foot since I last saw you."

"Are you gonna stay this time, or run away like a rat?" Andy asked.

Rachel felt her color rise since those had been her exact words in describing Micah.

"I plan to stay," he said, his voice gravelly.

Since his head was bent toward her son, his hat hiding his face, Rachel couldn't see Micah's expression.

Andy evidently took that for a promise because he said, "Good." Wiggling out of Micah's arms, he headed back toward Rachel. "I want a peanut butter sandwich for my snack. Okay, Mom?"

"Carrots, too?"

He grinned, pressing his tongue against one of his loose front teeth. "Maybe if I bite hard, my tooth will come out sooner."

"Maybe," she agreed handing him the keys to the back door, her attention caught by the vivid blue eyes of the man with Micah. Vivid and cold.

"This is Special Agent Flannery Kelmen," Micah said.

The man stepped forward, his handshake as brisk and no-nonsense as the expression in his eyes. "I met you briefly last spring."

"I remember." Everything then about the man's demeanor had been intimidating. It wasn't a lot better now.

He glanced back at the street, then nodded toward the back door that Andy was unlocking. "Maybe we could go inside?"

Though voiced as a question, Rachel was positive it was a command. "Of course."

The next few minutes were taken up with making Andy's snack and offering tea that they didn't want to the others. Micah was mostly quiet, his eyes never quite meeting hers, which set Rachel's nerves on edge. After Erin professed wanting to see a Lego tower that Andy was building, the two of them disappeared upstairs.

Rachel cleared her throat. "Since you all are here, it looks like things are in place for the safe house. What's next?"

Kelmen met her gaze straight-on. "The primary focus of this mission is to finish the job, and you're the key to tying together all the evidence we've gathered against Simon Graden."

He paused while Rachel looked from him to Micah, whose dark eyes steadily locked with hers, an expression there she couldn't define. Then he looked away, and the knots in her stomach began churning.

She replayed what Kelmen had just said. "There's no safe house, is there?" Her lips felt numb.

Micah shook his head, his expression unreadable, his dark eyes once again not quite meeting hers.

"You're going to help us take down Simon Graden," Kelmen said, drawing her attention, his eyes on hers, his tone matter-of-fact. "Given the business he's in, the half-million dollars he wants from you is small potatoes, but something about it is personal and has made him reckless. So we're going to take advantage of that."

"We?" Rachel began to tremble, and a roar echoed in her ears as she looked back at Micah. "You've lied to me again, Agent McLeod." She gestured angrily to the door. "Get out. All of you."

"Nice bravado." Kelmen smiled at Rachel, though there wasn't a single warm thing about the expression. "But we aren't going anywhere until this case is closed."

FIVE

Rachel shook her head against the suffocating pressure in her chest. "Wrong. My children's safety comes first—"

"Your children are in no danger, Mrs. Neesham. We'll see to that. What we need from you is to maintain contact with Graden until we can bring him in."

"And just how are you going to manage that little feat when you didn't get it done with a major investigation last spring?"

Kelmen smiled. "Simple. He wants something from you, and you're going to help us by pretending you have it."

"No," she said, remembering how intimidated she'd been the last time Kelmen interrogated her. *Not this time.* "I'm not. First of all, I don't have his money. And secondly, the one thing I wanted from you you've decided you won't give me."

He nodded once as though having made a decision, then he stood. "Suit yourself. If Graden is so positive you have his money, why should I believe that you don't? Men like him don't make mistakes like that."

Rachel stared at the man, sorting through what he was saying, what Micah had told her. Her attention shifted to him. "You told me I wasn't a suspect, and I believed you." She pressed a hand against her head. "Fool me once, shame on you. Fool me twice, shame on me." She waved toward the door. "Leave. Just leave." She met Kelmen's gaze. "And if any of you come back, it had better be with a warrant."

"Rachel," Micah said.

She turned on him, her expression fierce. Everything about her was so rigid, she looked as though she might shatter. He was hanging onto his own control by a thread, sucker-punched by Kelmen's unexpected change in tactics and buried alive by Rachel's belief that he had lied to her again. Of course, she believed it. Every revelation of the last few minutes confirmed it.

Except that he *hadn't* lied.

A lifetime ago when he had gone into law enforcement and then become a DEA agent, his reasons had been clear-cut. Simple. Put away the bad guys, like the one who had sold drugs to his best friend who had killed himself while hallucinating. Micah had seen his work as a DEA agent as a calling, God's hand guiding him as surely as any minister of faith. But things had stopped being simple the day he had met Rachel. Get the bad guy…and look like one himself. Get the bad guy…and destroy everything good for a woman whose only crime was to be a friend.

He held her gaze a long time, drowning in the knowledge that the second chance he had hoped for had disappeared with her trust.

"Come on, McLeod," Kelmen said, heading for the front of the house and calling up the stairs, "Asher, let's get going."

Finally, Rachel met Micah's gaze. He said, "I'm sorry."

She turned her back, her silence more telling than words.

Feeling like a man on the way to the gallows, Micah followed Erin Asher and Kelmen out the front door. Kelmen got in the sedan he and Erin had arrived in and drove away, leaving her to ride with Micah.

"I take it things didn't go real well," Erin said as they got into his Jeep Wrangler.

"And the sky is blue," Micah returned, jamming the key into the ignition and starting the vehicle. He cast one last look at the house. Andy was framed by the front door, his small face far too serious for a five-year-old. He gave a tiny wave, and Micah, his heart aching, waved back.

He'd been so sure Kelmen would agree to his plan. Get Rachel and her kids to safety, then close in on Graden. The threats to Rachel were enough probable cause to get a warrant to search Graden's house and office. Kelmen's objection had been they'd have the man on an extortion charge rather than the bigger charges required to topple his distribution network.

Micah understood the logic, but for the first time in his professional career, his concern was for the victims of the crime, not the perpetrators.

"Rachel Neesham wasn't quite what I expected," Erin was saying. "The woman looks as though a breeze could topple her over."

"She's stronger than she looks." There'd been nothing weak about her steely resolve when she had kicked them out of the house, and Micah admired her for it even as he worried about her being alone without any protection. His quick prayer for her safety was as automatic as driving a car.

"You gonna tell me what happened, or do I have to play twenty questions?"

Micah shot Erin a look, then grinned in spite of his sour mood. The frustration in her voice and the echo of his question to Rachel last night—had it only been last night?—brought home to him how thwarted he'd felt at every turn. He related the bare bones of the conversation, ending with "Kelmen has changed his mind about the safe house. He wants to use Rachel as bait."

"Really? Then what in the world am I doing here?"

Micah had no answer for that. His plan had called for Erin to act as a decoy for Rachel. Another agent, Nico Martinez, was supposed to escort the whole family to the safe house and stay with them. As far as Micah knew, Nico was on his way here. Micah knew from working with Kelmen on other cases that the man was a brilliant strategist, so knew he had a plan, even if he hadn't shared the details yet. But that didn't keep Micah from being furious over his treatment of Rachel.

Erin's cell phone rang, and her answer indicated Kelmen was on the other end of the line. The call ended in less than ten seconds. "He wants to meet us at Victorian Rose."

"Rachel's old shop," Micah murmured.

Ten minutes later, he drove to the rear of the store, which had a small dock. In his mind's eye, he saw it as it had been when he first came here last spring, the double doors wide open and Rachel supervising the careful unpacking of a seventeenth-century Italian credenza, which had eventually ended up in a celebrity's study in Aspen.

Micah parked next to Kelmen's car, then climbed the stairs next to the dock. Erin followed him into the building, where their footsteps echoed as they made their way through the gloomy workroom toward the front of the empty, bleak store.

Kelmen stood just inside the shadow line in front of the plate-glass window that looked out to the street. "How long do you think it will be before Graden makes his move on her?"

"We both know the answer to that," Micah said. "Any minute. And now she's there to deal with it alone."

"Nico's keeping an eye out," Kelmen said.

"She's still alone." So Nico *was* here. The fact that he'd checked in with Kelmen grated, even though Micah knew that Kelmen was the agent in charge.

"You need to get your emotions out of the way, Agent McLeod." Kelmen shot him a sideways look. "It's clear as day how you feel about her. Wearing your heart on your sleeve isn't going to get her out of the pickle she's in, nor is it going to put a lid on Graden."

"Leaving her high and dry wasn't part of the plan," Micah said through gritted teeth.

"If you were Graden, what would you do next?" Kelmen asked, his gaze going from Micah to Erin.

"He's got to look at her jobs and put two and two together," Erin said. "It's clear she doesn't have his half-million dollars."

"Or maybe she's simply waiting until things cool off and she can spend his money without getting caught," Kelmen said.

"Not possible," Micah stated flatly, wondering if Kelmen really believed what he was saying. "She doesn't have it. If she did, she would have turned it over to us."

"I've read the file," Erin said. "I agree. There's nothing in her background pointing to a single dishonest thing—not even a speeding ticket."

"Now that Graden has threatened her family and she's scared, he'll figure he has her backed into a corner," Micah said. "And, threatening to hurt her kids is just as powerful as doing anything to them, so…" A lightbulb flashed in Micah's head, and he hated the direction his thoughts took. "He'll tell her she can earn her way out of the problem, except we all know that once you step onto that slippery slope, there's no way out."

"And then we'll have him," Kelmen said, his hard face easing into a smile. "At last, we'll have him."

"This was *your* plan?" Micah asked.

"She'll have so much pressure on her, she'll have no recourse but to cooperate with us."

"She was already there," Micah returned. "Your scare tactics—"

"Worked." Walking away, Kelmen added, "And now you have another chance to elicit her cooperation."

Sure, Micah thought bitterly. This was only asking the impossible since trust between himself and Rachel was now irrevocably broken.

Now what? Rachel thought. Her whole world had been turned upside down again, all in the span of twenty minutes. She'd spent the day planning activities for Sarah and Andy while they were at the safe house, deciding that it would be a time to build memories. A time that would mark the beginning of their road back.

Now, she felt as though she had fallen into the center of a gaping void, like one of those black holes whose gravity was so dense even light could not escape.

Now what?

Last night Micah had agreed that leaving was a good idea. The pain that came with thinking about him made her press her hand to her head.

"Micah left without saying goodbye," Andy said.

Rachel opened her eyes and realized her son was standing in front of her with his hands crossed over his chest, his chin jutting out.

"And, he promised that he'd stay this time."

"I know, baby." She pulled her son onto her lap.

"I'm not a baby anymore, Mom," he said, squirming to get away. "I'm a big boy."

"Yes, you are."

"Do you know Micah's phone number? I want to call him and tell him to come back."

Rachel closed her eyes against the plaintive note in

her son's voice that matched the cadence in her heart. That's one more thing you owe me, Micah McLeod, she thought fiercely. No one hurts my children.

She cleared her throat. "He has other things to do right now."

"Maybe later?"

"I don't think so." She leaned back so she could see Andy's face and did her best to smile. "Because later…later, we're going to be on a trip with Sarah and Grandpa."

Andy looked dubiously at her. "What kind of trip? I don't want to go on any curvy roads 'cause I get car sick."

"It's a surprise. And what we need to do just as soon as Sarah gets home from school is go see Grandpa to arrange the final details."

"This is all pretty sudden, Mom," he said, sounding like an adult instead of a five-year-old. The cadence in his voice made him sound like his grandfather. "What about school? You always tell me going to school every day is very, very important."

"And it is." Rachel stood and headed to the phone where she kept a pad of paper. Time to make a list instead of wallowing around, bemoaning what she couldn't have instead of what she did. Raise some cash. And the only way to do that was to sell the heirlooms her grandmother had given her, furniture that had been in the family for at least five generations.

Carla Anderson had been telling her for months that she'd buy the mahogany Victorian renaissance console that was in the front entry. Rachel had been sure she'd never part with it, a piece of her past that represented everything she had wanted for her life. The money, though, would give them enough to live on for a few months if she was frugal.

And then what?

The question still plagued her long after she made the call to Carla and hours after Sarah came home from school. The question kept echoing through her head when she put the kids in the car and headed for her dad's house.

Somehow she had to have enough of a truce with him that she could talk him into coming with her and the children. Since he had been in the picture that Graden had taken, he was at risk just as much as her children.

"Grandpa won't be there," Sarah reminded her from the back seat after Rachel had turned onto his street. "Today's the day he takes care of the rose garden at the church. Remember?"

Rachel looked in the rearview mirror to the back seat. "I'd forgotten."

"That's 'cause she's distracted," Andy said. "And sad because Micah left without saying goodbye."

"Distracted," Rachel automatically corrected, her thoughts avoiding the mention of Micah and her gaze going from her daughter to the traffic behind her…and the gray car following her. Had it been there when she was driving down Main Street? She had the feeling it had been and hated that she couldn't remember for sure. When she turned at the next corner to double back to Grace Community Church, the car kept going, and she breathed a sigh of relief that only her imagination was chasing her.

When her attention again focused on the mundane business of driving, she realized her children were discussing Micah in quiet whispers and sending furtive glances in her direction. They'd both been so glad to see him, and his departure probably had them confused. Upset. And somehow, she'd have to figure out how to explain. Once more, she wished she had never brought him home that first evening last spring. He was the last thing she and her children needed.

She turned into the parking lot behind the church and found her dad's car in its usual parking place, though she didn't see him in the rose garden. Complete with a small gurgling fountain and a couple of benches, it was the perfect spot for prayer and reflection. It *had* been, she corrected herself. Prayer no longer provided hope or comfort, and her reflections these days were so melancholy, she didn't want to spend any time thinking.

After they got out of the car, the kids skipped ahead, ready to go into the church since her dad wasn't outside. Sarah held open the door and waited for Andy to go through it, calling, "Grandpa, where are you?"

Rachel followed them inside, coming to a stop in the vestibule. The sanctuary was in front of her and a hallway to her right led toward the classrooms and Reverend Staum's office—it had been her father's before he retired. The kids had headed down the hallway, and she could hear their voices echoing in the quiet building.

She went to the doorway of the sanctuary and looked

in. The afternoon sun streamed through the stained-glass windows and bathed the white walls in a kaleidoscope of color. And she wanted to lay down her head and howl because the comfort she'd sensed for most of her life was nowhere to be found now.

Leaving the sanctuary, she headed for the minister's office, knowing that her dad and Reverend Staum were likely engaged in a lively discussion over some esoteric point of theology. She knocked on the door and was summoned in.

"Rachel." Reverend Staum greeted her. He got up from his desk and gave her a quick hug. "You don't know how glad I am to see you. Your dad was telling me that you are giving some thought to selling your house."

"I…" Her voice trailed away. It was true. She *had* been thinking about it, but actually doing it, she hated to even consider it. From the day she had bought it, the huge rooms and big windows had made it immediately feel like home. When she and her husband had moved in, they had talked about growing old there, of having family celebrations in the sprawling yard. The last one had been his funeral.

Then she had dreamed of turning the house into a bed and breakfast, and had been diligently saving her money toward that end.

The reverend patted her hand. "From your expression, I think I must have misunderstood."

Rachel shrugged. "If things don't turn around financially for me soon, I may have to sell it."

"But you don't want to."

She shook her head. "No, I don't want to."

He took both of her hands within his. "If you change your mind, you'll call me, won't you? It would be a perfect home for us."

Too easily she imagined the reverend and his family in the house. With his five children, they needed the space. In fact, the attic could be remodeled so each child could have a bedroom. That would allow him to turn the downstairs bedroom that had originally been a parlor into a study.

Perfect as it sounded for him, the thought brought a lump to her throat.

She squeezed his hands, then let them go. "I promise. You'll be the first person I call."

"And now, what brings you to the church?"

"I was looking for my dad. His car is here, but I can't find him."

"I haven't seen him, but he's got to be close by." Reverend Staum glanced back toward the desk. "And I must get back to my sermon."

"I'll leave you to it, then."

"God bless you," he said by way of goodbye.

Rachel headed toward the front of the building and the main entrance to the church. The door opened, and she called out, sure this must be her dad. The man's face was hidden for an instant by the bright light behind him until the door closed. And then, Simon Graden stood in front of her, as though created from her worst fears. An evil presence in this sacred place.

Her heart lurched into her throat. "Where is my father?"

Graden smiled. "You're getting better. That's the right question." He came to stand beside her and peer into the sanctuary. "Nice, though a little on the shabby side."

Her pulse galloping, Rachel listened for her children who were still somewhere in the back of the building, wanting to keep this man away from them, wanting to know where her father was, wanting to know what Graden was doing here…wanting the too-familiar panic to subside so she could think.

"Where is my father?" she repeated, hating that her voice sounded like a croak.

"He'll be along soon," Graden said, stepping into the church and looking around. "He's picking up a tree from the nursery—I'm donating it in memory of my younger sister."

"His car is here."

Graden gave her an amused glance. "Now, Rachel, a tree wouldn't very well fit in his car, would it? That's why he went with my driver."

Down the hall, the chattering of her children grew louder, and a second later they turned the corner and came into view.

Next to her, Graden smiled once more, and came out of the church to stand with her in the vestibule. "Ah. Your children are just adorable."

"Mom, we can't find Grandpa anywhere," Andy said.

The fretful note in his voice magnified her own worry a thousand times.

"We looked everywhere," Sarah added.

"Who are you?" Andy asked Graden.

"Simon Graden," he said. "I'm a friend of your mother's."

No, you're not. Not now, not ever. "We were just finishing up," Rachel said, somehow sounding normal. "Why don't you two wait for me outside?" She waved in the direction of the rose garden. "Over by the fountain where I can see you."

For once, the two of them went without giving her any argument. The minute they were out of earshot, she looked back at Graden, who was still watching her with that pseudo-sophisticated smile.

"You are not a friend," she said, spacing the words. "And you *will* stay away from my children."

"Business acquaintance, then," he agreed with a negligent shrug. "A far better description."

"I don't see how."

"Don't be flip, Rachel. You can't afford it. Since I'm a reasonable man, I'm here to make you an offer—a chance for you to make restitution."

With awful clarity, she suspected what he would might say next.

"You'll take care of running some…" He paused, as though thinking of the right word, then snapped his fingers. "…Errands for me. And, in exchange, after a time, we'll consider your debt repaid."

"There is no debt." She could only imagine the errands he had for her. She also knew the "debt" would never be repaid.

He continued as if she hadn't spoken. "You can either pay up now or work your way out of the problem.

You know Tommy Manderoll?" he asked, and before she could answer, added, "Of course, you do—he was Angela's boyfriend. As I was saying, you'll meet Tommy tomorrow at that pool hall he's so fond of, and he'll tell you what to do. He'll be waiting for you at eleven-thirty."

"I'll be at work then." Rachel shook her head, not so much in refusal, but in complete disbelief at being ordered around.

"This wasn't a request."

Outside, Rachel saw an oversize pickup come into the parking lot, a large tree extending over the tailgate. Her dad and another man were in the cab of the vehicle. He got out of the truck, looking not only unharmed, but relaxed. Her children ran over to him, while the other man let down the tailgate and pulled the tree from the pickup bed.

Some of the tension in her shoulders eased.

"See," Graden said. "I told you the truth." When she looked back at him, he added, "You can count on me to tell you the truth, Rachel."

The truth! A hysterical bubble formed in the middle of her chest, threatening to explode. She'd been wanting the truth, demanding it, and here it was.

"And the truth is," Graden continued, his gaze on the unloading of the tree, "that I'm no longer a stranger to your children, someone who should be avoided. I'm no longer a stranger to your father. Do you understand what I'm saying?"

She did. He could get to them anytime he wanted.

SIX

Graden held the door for Rachel so she could precede him outside, as though he somehow knew that she'd go without making a scene. Her father saw them and waved.

Just as had happened with Jane, everything on the surface was normal.

"Very good, Rachel," Graden said softly to her. "Now all you have to do is hold up your end of the bargain so my man doesn't find it necessary to use that shovel for anything other than digging."

She looked ahead and saw the driver of the truck was using a spade to enlarge the hole where the tree was to be planted. Andy was squatted next to the hole, and though Rachel couldn't hear him, she knew he was asking his mile-a-minute questions. Sarah stood next to her grandpa, one hand on the slender trunk of the tree. A perfectly ordinary scene but for Graden's sinister presence.

Graden strolled toward her father and she followed in his wake, everything in his manner conveying his confidence that everything was going according to his plan.

Her father stepped around Graden and, as was his custom despite their rift, gave her a warm hug. She fiercely hugged him back, feeling as she had when she'd been ten and positive her dad could fix anything. Except she wasn't ten and he couldn't fix this.

When her father stepped away, Graden said, "I'm so glad you had time to go get the tree this afternoon. You don't know how much it means to me to know that I'll have a living memorial to my mother."

"I thought it was your sister," Rachel said instead of screaming to her father to take her children and run.

Once more Graden turned his attention on her, that smile not faltering a bit. "How kind of you to remember," he said, turning back to her father, his voice and expression turning somber. "I'm afraid I bent your daughter's ear far too long with the sad story of how my sister was led astray by a drug runner who killed her after he found out she was cooperating with the police." He grasped the trunk of the tree they had taken from the back of the pickup. "This is a flowering crab-apple, right?"

Once more, she recognized the threat within his glib lie. Rachel thrust her hands into the pockets of her sweater to hide their trembling.

"It is," her father said. "Just as you ordered, though it would have been nice if you'd told me the nursery was in Rifle."

They had been all the way to Rifle? Rachel wondered. That was nearly forty miles from Carbondale. Why had they gone so far when there were numerous nurseries right here or in Glenwood Springs?

"Would there be room here for another? For my mother?" Graden asked.

"We're more than happy to have this wonderful gift, which deserves more recognition than a private thank you. We need to get together with Reverend Staum and set up a time for the dedication service," her father said.

Rachel's thoughts, though, remained fixed on the drive her dad had been on. Too many deserted miles between here and there with a dozen places along the way that he could have been murdered and his body dumped. She shivered even though she was standing in the sunshine.

They talked only a few minutes longer while Rachel studied them all, her children within arm's reach of Graden, her dad's earnest appreciation of the man and his gift and his open empathy for Graden's sister. The driver, who had pulled the burlap from around the root ball and moved the tree into its newly dug hole as though it weighed nothing. And Graden, ingratiating himself with her family.

And all she seemed capable of was standing here like one of the townsfolk admiring the emperor's nonexistent new clothes.

Finally, Graden said goodbye, but not before pulling magic coins out of first Sarah's ear and then Andy's. Then he came back to Rachel, taking both of her hands and whispering to her, "Don't disappoint me, Rachel."

Then they left, Graden waving like an old friend. And the afternoon sun was still shining, and her dad was beaming.

Despite the strain that had been between them, he kissed her cheek and said, "Come sit with me."

She followed him, her attention on her children who were playing a few yards away. The clear goals she'd had on the way here had been lost beneath another quicksand change.

"Your emotions are always plain as day on your face," he said. "This is the first time you've been here in nearly six months, but I don't think that's why you look like you've seen a ghost. What exactly happened between you and Simon Graden?"

She turned her head and looked at her father. His hazel eyes held compassion, as always. But that didn't mean the gulf between them had been bridged.

Don't make me hurt them. Graden's whispered admonition raced through her mind, juxtaposed with the stronger need to tell her father the truth. They hadn't said much more than "Hello, nice weather," for several weeks, and now the things she needed to say to him were so enormous, she didn't even know where to start.

"You know that demand for the half-million dollars?" she blurted. "He's the one asking for it."

"You're sure about this?" Her father's gaze was direct when he added, "That's a huge accusation to make—"

"He shook me down for the money right before you got here, so yes, I'm positive."

"But you didn't say anything—"

"Because he said he'd hurt you." She waved to encompass Sarah and Andy who were playing in the water coming out of the trickling fountain. "That act he does, talking all nice to everyone—it's just that,

Dad. An act. He wants his money, or…" The enormity of the "or" made her voice clog. She took a deep breath. "The point is—the reason I'm here is we need to go into hiding and get away—"

"Hiding? Running away?"

"Hiding, yes, Dad, hiding."

"And what kind of business is he in?"

"I don't know, except that the DEA—"

"There's your answer. You should call that McLeod fellow who was here last spring. Surely he'll do whatever is necessary to make sure you and the children are taken care of."

"I've already talked to him, Dad, and they're not going to be any help."

"What do you mean by that?" He sounded as bewildered and indignant as she had felt.

"Just that. I've talked to Micah several times now." She didn't see any point in telling her dad that Micah had twice promised his help. And then he'd done the usual about-face, reminding her of how he had turned on her last spring. "His agenda is to get his man, and that doesn't include taking care of us."

Her father sat staring into space, and she wished he would say something. Anything. Her face might reveal her emotions and what she was thinking, but for all her life, she had never been able to read her father's face. She was sure that he was troubled, maybe even upset, but nothing in his expression gave her a clue.

"Running away is never the way to solve a problem," he finally said. "You face things straight on."

Rachel rose from the chair, raking a hand through

her hair, wishing she knew how to get him to see things her way just this once. "Not this time."

"Where would you go?" he pointed out. "For how long? And always looking over your shoulder, always being afraid. That's no way for Andy and Sarah to live."

In that, Rachel agreed with him. Her gaze went to her children, who were skipping around the newly planted tree. "At least they'll be safe."

"I'm still trying to imagine that amiable man being any real danger to you. If this is a debt from the store—"

"Dad."

"Let me finish. Talk to him. If he's a businessman, he knows that sometimes there's a risk. After you declare bankruptcy, this will be one of the debts you include—"

"It's not like that, Dad. I think this has something do with Angela."

"Why would you think that?"

"Because I went to the prison and asked her. She denied it, but then she called Micah. Why would she do that if she wasn't involved?"

Her father pinned her with the look that always made her squirm. "She's not here to defend herself—"

"You can believe her, but you can't believe me." Sudden anger swamped her, and she strode away a couple of steps, then came back. "That's not real reassuring, Dad." She glanced back at her children. "If you won't come with us, fine." With that she headed for the car. "Go kiss your grandpa goodbye," she called to the children. "It's time for us to go."

"Rachel." Within his voice, she heard the same plea that had been in Micah's not two hours ago.

She turned back around. "If you change your mind, call me. I've gotta go." She waved a hand. "Things to do and all that."

She slipped behind the wheel, lost all over again that she and her dad were still a continent apart in their understanding of each other. He hugged both her children, and she felt so separated from them all, she wanted to cry.

The sun was going down when Micah arrived at Chester Holt's house. Before getting out of the car, he took in the view, which was as good as it got, in his opinion. To the south of town, Mount Sophris was bathed in brilliant light, snow gleaming in the crevices near the summit. Still surprised that Rachel's father had called him, Micah looked toward the house where a movement in the front window snagged his attention. Picking his hat off the seat, Micah opened the door and got out. He was halfway to the door when Reverend Chester Holt opened it and came outside.

"It can't be a coincidence that you're in town when I called you," he said.

"It's not." Micah extended his hand. "It's nice to see you." He'd liked Rachel's father from the first time they'd met, the man's expression usually open, often smiling. Today, though, his expression was as somber as a judge.

The man didn't take his hand, but stood with his arms folded over his chest. "Just so we're straight. My daughter says she asked for your help and you refused to give it."

"*Refused* isn't exactly the right word." Micah was glad that she had gone to see her father even though he was pretty sure the corner she'd been backed into was the reason.

Chester's expression became a glower. "The English language is rich with words. So pick the right one."

Micah took off his hat and fingered the brim. "A misunderstanding. Rachel's safety, and Sarah's and Andy's, too, is everything to me." Their eyes locked, and he added, "I don't like what's happened to her one bit."

Her father's expression eased a bit. "Well, then. Maybe it's nice to see you, too." He motioned for Micah to follow him and they went up a walkway along the side of the house that was lined with flowers in colorful, lush bloom. A patio with an umbrella-covered table and chairs was at the back of the house.

"You don't look much worse for the wear," Chester said.

Unlike Rachel, Micah thought, who had lost weight and whose eyes no longer sparkled.

Chester motioned toward one of the chairs.

"Want a lemonade or an iced tea?"

Micah shook his head. "What did you want to see me about?"

Chester sat down on one of the chairs, the umbrella casting a shadow across his face and making him look old, tired.

Feeling as though he was looming over the man and, therefore, doing nothing to ease the tension in Chester's expression, Micah sat down on another chair and looked out at the yard. Long shadows from the neighbor's house stretched across the ground.

"You left a pretty wide wake in your departure," Chester said.

The statement was said without heat, but Micah heard criticism, anyway. He deserved every bit of it. The oblique observation didn't get anywhere close to letting him know why Rachel's father had called.

"My grandchildren talk about you all the time, and I know little Sarah, in particular, was seeing you as a possible daddy."

The knife in Micah's conscience twisted.

"And Rachel. She doesn't talk about you at all, and I figured she hadn't spoken with you until your name came up today." Finally Chester turned his head and looked at him. "My girl is scared. She's ready to run away with my grandchildren." He took a breath. "You do this for a living, Special Agent McLeod. Is the danger as real as she believes?"

Micah nodded.

"You know, and you're not removing her from it? Why?"

Weighing the "why," Micah didn't have an immediate answer. Saying that Rachel had kicked him out would sound like the feeble excuse that it was.

Once more staring straight ahead, Chester said, "The unanswerable why. I should have figured that, since 'why' is the question I'm least able to answer, as well. Wouldn't it be nice if a bully was as recognizable as Goliath was to David? Dealing with him when he comes bearing gifts, that's a harder thing."

"Who brought you gifts?" Micah asked, the hair on the back of his neck rising.

"Simon Graden. I think you know him."

"We've never met," Micah said, his voice rough. "Maybe you'd like to be a whole lot more direct."

"I got a call this morning from a man who told me he thought the garden at our church was the prettiest he had ever seen, and that seemed to him like a message from God because he'd been looking for a place to plant a tree in memory of his mother. He had the tree picked out, and asked if I could come with him to the nursery. Little did I know at the time that the nursery was nearly halfway to Grand Junction. Except, after he and a man with the strange name of Two-bits—"

"Two-bits Perez?" Micah interrupted, all the concern about Rachel's father having been lured into a vehicle alone coming to a pinpoint. Two-bits Perez was the snitch Micah had used last spring. "About forty, with dark hair and eyes and the physique of a body builder?"

"That's the man." Chester looked at Micah. "How much more of this story do you want me to tell?"

"How about I fill in the blanks?" Micah said. "You and Two-bits went to get the tree, and Graden stayed behind. Was there really a tree?"

"There was, and we planted it on the church grounds. When we got back there, Rachel was there with her children and Mr. Graden."

"Was she hurt?" Micah surged from the chair.

"No. Pale. Scared, but not physically hurt." Chester shook his head. "I knew something was wrong, though. She told me that you know about the extortion—"

"That's right."

"And you refused to help her?" Her father's voice was rough now, his eyes bright. "Maybe she has the right of it. Maybe running—"

"Isn't the answer. Not alone. Not without protection." Micah turned away from her father and stared out at the skyline where the last rays of the sun were blazing from the horizon. "The original plan had been to get her to a safe house, but that was scrapped."

"That isn't real reassuring." Chester stood and came to stand next to him. "If even half of what my daughter told me today is true, then you have some work to do, Special Agent. As her father…" He choked up suddenly, and he took a breath. "You always want to stand between your child and any possible hurt. The scraped knee when she's seven, the first love who breaks her heart when she's fourteen, the death of her husband." He turned his head and looked at Micah. "Those are nothing compared to the hurt she's experiencing now. I can't shield her from it or fix it. She's not thinking clearly, and she's poised to run. I'm begging you, McLeod, if that's what it takes. Help us. Help her."

He had come here with exactly that intention, and somehow the plan had derailed itself. That was being too generous. The plan had gone south because he hadn't stuck to his guns about Rachel needing protection. He'd dumped his better judgment and years of experience in deference to a fellow agent whose record was no more stellar than his own.

"I need to know that you can take this on, McLeod.

This is a battle my daughter is not equipped to handle on her own."

"No, it's not." Frustration made Micah's voice rough.

"You once told me that you were a man of faith even though you didn't think of yourself as religious."

"That's true."

"Personally, I've never quite understood the difference, but the one thing I know for sure is that the only way to live life is to move forward in faith."

"Ask for in faith, as though the thing is already done," Micah said, the words an echo to his morning prayer that had crumbled into bits when Rachel told them all to leave a few hours ago. He met her father's gaze. "Easier said than done some days."

"Perhaps you're too close to the situation, too emotionally involved, to see clearly."

It was such an echo of what Kelmen had told him that Micah felt the knife in his conscience twist once more. He'd come because he wanted to be close to Rachel, because he'd been emotionally involved from the day he had met her. To hear from both his supervising officer and her father that he'd failed her because he was too close...

"If I'm the problem, there are other qualified agents." It was on the tip of his tongue to confess that he no longer trusted his ability to set Rachel's situation right.

"Maybe," Chester agreed, "but I believe you're here for a bigger purpose. It's no coincidence things came about today as they did or that I had saved your card." His eyes bright with resolve, he stood, and motioned for Micah to join him. "There's something I want you to see."

Chester led the way toward the back of the yard where a bush grew close to the garage. He pointed at the space between the garage and the bush, and said, "Tell me what you see."

At first, Micah didn't see anything. Then, he noticed a geometric spider's web stretched between the eave of the building and the branches, the spider itself resting the in the center of the web. It swayed gently in the breeze.

"When the wind blows the web down, less than a day passes before the spider rebuilds it again. That says something about perseverance, but that's not the point."

Micah studied the web, waiting for the rest of it.

"What would happen if you told the spider to put the silk back inside itself—assuming you could make yourself understood. Could it do it?"

Micah shook his head.

"In fact, we've both watched a spider drop from a ceiling, spinning a strand that could be ten or twelve feet, made all within a few seconds. And every time I see it, I wonder. Where did the silk come from?" He paused. "From the spider, clearly. But, once the silk is out, it can't go back into its body. My hunch is that if you could somehow pack it all together, the sum of it would be greater than the spider itself."

Micah looked at the web again, appreciating it in a way.

"We're like that," Chester said. "Capable of deeds greater than we know we can do, bigger than ourselves." He clapped a hand on Micah's shoulder.

"Whatever your fears, I know you have the wisdom and experience and worldly knowledge to see through this task that you left unfinished last spring. That's why you're back—to finish whatever it is that hangs between you and my daughter."

SEVEN

At that same moment, Rachel was listening to the phone message left by Carla Anderson. She wouldn't be buying the mahogany console after all. Though she loved it, they had just paid the college tuition bill for their son, and an extra five thousand for the console wasn't in the budget. Maybe by springtime, though.

Can nothing go my way? Rachel wondered as she set down the receiver and turned her attention back to their dinner.

"Where are we going on our trip?" Andy asked. He was setting the table, arranging the silverware on each side of the plate as he had been taught. He grinned when she looked at him. "I think we *need* to go to Disneyland."

"Need, hmm?" Pushing this latest setback to the rear of her mind, Rachel poured each of them a glass of milk. "Not this time."

"I don't want to miss any school," Sarah said, carefully carrying the glasses to the table. "But since we're studying marine mammals right now, maybe Sea World would be a good idea."

"And what do you know about marine mammals?" Rachel set the macaroni and cheese in the center of the table along with a bowl of fresh green beans from the garden.

"That's what they're called. Whales and dolphins and even sea otters. Oh, Mom, you should see the pictures. They are so cute." And she was off, relating the things she had learned in school, talking a mile a minute. Andy added his two cents' worth, and the trip was forgotten, at least for the moment.

The trip that Rachel had no idea how to make happen. *You face things straight on,* her dad's voice echoed in her head. Graden's demands and Kelmen's suspicions had her backed into a corner, so there wasn't much choice but to face them unless she intended to cower with her back turned.

They sat down to eat, and Rachel asked, "Who's turn for grace tonight?"

"Yours," Sarah said to Andy, who was also saying, "Yours!"

"Decide," Rachel said.

"I think you should say grace." Sarah's gaze locked with Rachel's.

"Yeah," Andy piped in. "Like you used to." He gave her one of his beguiling smiles. "I like your prayers, Mom."

Her heart suddenly pounding, she looked from one child to the other. She had never told them that she had stopped praying, but had simply gone along with the usual patterns of their life and encouraged them to say grace at mealtime, prayers at bedtime. This was the first time they had confronted her about it, though neither one could possibly know.

Sarah took her hand and squeezed. "I think Andy's right."

Taking her son's hand as well, Rachel bowed her head, tears burning at the back of her eyes, her throat so clogged that she could barely breathe, much less speak. "Heavenly father," she murmured. Then what? With a lifelong habit, the words should have been at the tip of her tongue, but they weren't.

A long second passed, and then Sarah whispered, "You start with thank you, Mom. That's what Grandpa always says. Thank you for the blessings."

Rachel squeezed her daughter's hand back. "Thank you for the blessings that fill our lives. For this food. For one another." The unshed tears choked her, as she absorbed the truth of the words. She *was* thankful they had food to eat and one another to love. She took another deep breath, thinking *I could sure use some help to get out of this mess we're in. To keep Sarah and Andy and Dad safe. To keep me from losing my mind.*

"Amen," Andy finally whispered, as though prompting her.

"Amen." Rachel kept her head bowed for long seconds after the children let go of her hand.

"Why are you crying, Mom?" Andy asked, his voice matter of fact as he reached for the bowl of macaroni.

"I don't know." And that was the truth. Her heart felt as though its door had been pried open, revealing a tender and vulnerable center. Never before, even during the awful days right after her husband had died, had prayer left her feeling like this.

"Can we bake cookies after dinner?" Sarah dished herself up from the bowl her brother shoved across the table, then nudged it toward Rachel.

"It's a school night."

"But I thought we were going on a trip. And we need cookies for that."

"Yeah," Andy said with a grin as he methodically stabbed a stack of macaroni onto his fork. "*Need,* Mom."

"I've changed my mind about the trip," Rachel said. "So no cookies." She wasn't about to add that she didn't think there was enough butter or sugar to make them. Giving her daughter a bright smile, she added, "I like that you're excited about the things you're learning. Missing school would be a shame, right?"

"How 'bout pudding, then? We could make that fast," Sarah said. "And have some before bedtime."

They had a box of pudding. "We could," Rachel agreed with an inward smile. Her world had been rocked over a few simple words and her children had already moved onto the next mundane thing at hand. And that was a good thing, she decided.

With that, her thoughts once more went back to Simon Graden and his demands. Somehow, this time the fear wasn't quite so consuming and she actually felt as though she could solve this if she could simply get her thinking to quit going in circles.

As she supervised homework and bathtime, her thoughts continued to dwell on Graden's demands.

What if there really was money owed him? That

thought hit right after she put the kids to bed. Stunned by the idea, her ideas took off at a gallop. If there was, maybe it was in the pile of disorganized papers that had been left behind after the DEA took everything else. She'd thrown everything into a disorderly jumble of boxes at the back of the garage.

Making a last check on the kids and the securely locked front door, she headed outside where the night air had taken on a chilly edge. No doubt about it, summer was over. The first frost was probably only days away.

Looking back at the house, she went the few feet to the side door of the garage and flipped on the light. The heap of boxes at the back of the garage was as chaotic as she remembered. No easy way to get through the process, she thought, except start with the nearest box and work her way through them one by one. Leaving the door open so she could keep an eye on the back door and listen for the children, she set to work.

Sometime later, she couldn't have said how long, movement outside the door caught her attention, followed by a knock. Startled, but telling herself Graden...or his henchmen...weren't likely to be so gracious, she looked up, just as Micah McLeod came through the door, his Stetson in hand.

Her heart lurched at the sight of him.

Taking in the piles of boxes he said, "What are you doing here?"

"I might ask you the same thing."

He came farther into the garage. "I've been sitting in the car for the last hour mustering up enough courage to come see you."

She ought to be more angry at him, she decided. Startled, yes. Anger…somehow she couldn't summon that up. Maybe she was simply too tired.

"Your turn," he said. "What are you doing?"

"Looking for Graden's money." She glanced around at the mess. When the DEA had stripped the store, this was all that had been left. A few records that evidently had nothing to do with their investigation. A few boxes of bric-a-brac, a straight-back chair with a broken leg, and a Victorian fainting couch that had been stripped down to the springs in preparation for being reupholstered. Every time she had come in here, she'd been too upset and depressed to deal with figuring out what was left.

"What makes you think it might be here?" he asked, taking a seat on a good-sized box.

She shrugged, not feeling at all casual. "People don't usually do things out of the blue just to be contrary. If Graden thinks I have the money, he must have a reason to think so." She waved a hand to encompass the boxes. "So, I'm looking."

"If it were this simple, don't you think Graden would have already been here, searching?"

"I hadn't thought of that." She met Micah's gaze, the familiar jolt of awareness hitting once more in the middle of her chest and making her wish once more she really could trust the promises she always seemed to see in his eyes. The overwhelming sense of being dragged against her will swept through her once more. "I was just hoping. He told me that I need to go see Tommy Manderoll tomorrow, and he'll put me to work."

At the sheer misery in her tone and her eyes, Micah stood up and reached for her, pulling her off the box where she sat and into his arms. Wanting only to comfort her, he wrapped his arms around her. She stood rigid for a second, her spine as straight as her principles. At last, she sighed, and her posture softened as one arm came around his waist and her other hand tucked itself against his thundering heart.

A thousand thoughts ran through his mind, but the two that surfaced with any clarity were that this was the first time he had held her in his arms. The second was no one should be burdened with the level of stress she had been dealing with these last long weeks. The things he wanted to say to her, he couldn't. It wasn't the right time, even if he'd had a single illusion that she might believe him.

He hated knowing Graden had done exactly as Kelmen had predicted.

Finally, she sighed, her breath hot against his neck. Tipping his head, he laid his cheek against hers. A silent prayer welled from his heart, for her well being and for the safety of her children. For his ability to see her through this time and make sure she and her children came out the other side whole and happy.

"I think I'm supposed to be mad at you," she said softly.

"You have every reason." He loosened his hold on her so she could step away if she wanted, but she didn't. She didn't. If he were a less realistic kind of man, he might be tempted to think that meant something.

"Is it worth looking, or am I just wasting my time?"

"That all depends on the outcome," he said. "It isn't if we find Graden's money."

"We?"

"We." His arms tightened around her, and he pressed a kiss against her hair. "You're not in this alone, Rachel, no matter what it looked like this afternoon. I admit that I have a job to do, but you come first." He leaned back to meet her gaze. "I know you have zero reason to believe me, but you and the children are my first priority. Always."

She stepped back then, her gaze falling away from his.

"Tell me about—" When she looked at him, he discarded the question he'd been about to ask—the interrogator's question. Since he already knew most of the story, that would be treating her like a suspect. "I talked to your dad a couple of hours ago and he told me that you'd both seen Graden today. And that Graden had threatened you again." He took a breath.

"That must have been some conversation," she said, sinking back on the box where she'd been earlier, picking up a packet of envelopes that looked as though they might have contained bank statements.

"I mostly listened. Unfortunately, this is the corner Kelmen wanted you backed into." When she once again pinned him in place with her sad eyes, he added, "He didn't think you'd cooperate unless you were…" The right word failed him.

"Coerced?" she finally filled in.

"Yeah."

"What about you? Is that what you thought?"

"*No.*"

At his tone, she looked at him, then back at her task, her silky hair falling forward. "If I'm ever tempted to be nice to him, remind me that I don't like him."

Her head was bent, so he couldn't see her expression. But her tone was lighter, and for that Micah was thankful. Thankful, and unbearably tempted to ask if she liked *him*. Talk about juvenile, he thought. "Tell me what else Graden said."

She related that he wanted her to run some errands for him, the tone of her voice indicating she knew it was bad. Unfortunately, Micah had the frame of reference to know just how bad those errands could be. The task now was to get the job done with as minimal a risk to Rachel as possible.

"I have a plan," he said.

She looked up from the box she was sorting through, searched his eyes for a moment and then nodded.

"When are you supposed to meet Tommy?"

"Eleven-thirty."

"I had Erin—the agent who was here this afternoon—come because I hoped to have her stand in as a decoy for you."

"But Tommy knows me."

"He does. But, I can have Erin there, too, to give you backup."

"What if she's spotted?"

"She's a pro," Micah assured Rachel. "She won't be."

"And I just find out what Tommy wants me to do?" She sounded dubious, as though it couldn't be that simple.

"That's it. And then report back to me."

"You?" she asked. "Or Kelmen?"

"Me," he said firmly.

"And then what?"

"It all depends on Tommy and what he wants you to do."

"Will I have to wear a wire or anything like that?"

Micah grinned. "Nah. Erin will have a mike strong enough to pick up anything in the room. For this initial meeting, it'll be fine. You just need to be yourself."

"Sure," she drawled. "Just be myself. The preacher's daughter turned felon."

For the first time since he'd been back, Rachel's voice finally held a smile, however turned inward.

"That's the spirit," he said. "I knew you weren't out for the count just yet."

The following morning, Rachel walked through the door of Classic Billiards, which was between a craft store where she used to shop regularly and a bookstore where everyone knew her. She hoped she'd be able to get out of here without being seen. Given all the gossip there'd been about her after her store was shut down, she could only imagine what would be said about her hanging around a pool hall.

She'd been expecting someplace that matched the grimy sets of old movies, but this place looked like a library out of an English manor house. It reeked of smoke though, and she wrinkled her nose, looking around.

She didn't see Tommy. A couple of men playing at

a pool table near the rear of the room were being watched by a woman in tight jeans and black halter top. Rachel looked away, imagining too well what she did for a living. But something in the woman's posture made her look back. It was Erin Asher, and her gaze skipped right over Rachel as though they had never met.

Rachel looked away. Knowing she wasn't alone bolstered her courage, just as Micah had promised.

"You gonna stand there in the door, sweetheart, or come in?" The voice came from a heavyset man who was polishing glasses behind the bar.

Smoothing her hand against her skirt, Rachel stepped farther into the room. The door closed behind her with a thunk.

"Nobody's gonna bite you," the bartender added.

Lifting her chin, she crossed the deep-burgundy carpet. "I'm looking for Tommy Manderoll."

The bartender looked her up and down so thoroughly that she had to make sure she hadn't spilled something on her skirt or sweater.

"Honey, you're not his type."

"Nor would I want to be."

Her answer made the man grin. "Well now, it's a little early for him." Glancing at the clock, he said, "I expect he'll be along within the next hour."

She might have to wait here an *hour?*

"Can I get you something to drink while you wait?" he asked.

Rachel shot the man a glance that evidently matched her shocked reaction because he laughed.

"A soft drink or coffee?" he clarified.

"Coffee? Well, yes. That would be fine. With cream, if you have it." She headed for a table near the wall and sat down.

Still smiling to himself, he set a mug on the table in front of her and filled it, setting a few packages of half-and-half next to it. Hoping she didn't have to wait too long, Rachel stirred her coffee, covertly watching Erin, who had a can of soda and a straw that she occasionally sipped giving every impression that she was entranced by the game of pool going on.

A half hour later, Rachel decided she'd had enough. She paid the too-expensive price for the coffee and stood to leave. Just then, Tommy sauntered through the door as though he owned the place.

He grinned like an old friend. "I didn't think you'd come." He took off an expensive-looking leather sports coat and hung it over the back of the chair next to where Rachel had been sitting. "Bill, guys, I want you to meet my good friend Rachel Neesham."

"You're coming up in the world," Bill, the bartender, said, giving Rachel a wink.

Rachel supposed that was a compliment, but she didn't like it and she hated all the attention focused on her. Denying that Tommy was a friend of hers would undoubtedly sound stupid, so she didn't say anything.

Tommy took her by the arm to guide her back to the chair she had just vacated. She pulled away, staring at him, trying to remember why she had ever thought she had liked this man. She hadn't, she realized. She'd put up with him because Angela had liked him. Not that it had done her any good in the end. Tommy had made a deal to walk in exchange for turning over evidence that had made Angela plead guilty.

"Just tell me what you want me to do," Rachel said softly after seeing the bartender's attention was mostly on the television, "and I'll be on my way."

Tommy shook his head and brushed the hair away from his forehead where it perpetually fell over his eye. "Have a drink with me first."

"You know I don't drink."

"I'll have my usual," Tommy said to Bill without taking his eyes off Rachel. "And she'll have—"

"More coffee?" the bartender filled in.

She glanced at him and shook her head, then back at her clasped hands, remembering why she had come here. To gather information. Find out what Tommy wanted, and through that, a way to trap Graden and end her nightmare.

"Ever hear from Angela?" Tommy asked.

"I don't want to make small talk. I just want to find out what you—"

"I know what you want." Lowering his head close to hers, he whispered, "You don't actually think I'm going to tell you with all these people around, do you? Too many ears."

Rachel looked around. Except for the bartender, the pair of pool players at the back of the room and Erin, the place was empty.

Bill set down a fresh mug of coffee even though she hadn't asked for it, and a soft drink for Tommy. As if sensing her surprise that he wasn't drinking something stronger, he saluted her with the glass before taking a sip.

Then he picked it up and headed toward one of the pool tables, motioning her to follow him. Reluctantly she did.

Setting his glass down on a nearby table, he pulled a cue from the rack, his attention on the others in the room. Evidently satisfied they were all busy doing their own thing, he stepped close to her. So close, she could smell his cologne, which was too strong and a scent she would forever associate with this moment.

"Are you still working at one of those motels along the Interstate?"

"Assuming I haven't lost my job by being here instead of where I'm supposed to be."

Tommy clucked his tongue. "There you go again, seeing the small picture. You need to be thinking bigger. Then maybe you'll get to keep your house and enjoy all those fine things you used to have in the store."

He was baiting her, she knew he was. "You don't know anything about my house or what I like."

He leaned toward her. "I know that you're no better than the rest of us. You're here to make a buck any way you can. So, here's the deal. You're gonna call me later today and confirm that you are working tomorrow. And, in one of the rooms you clean, there'll be a package. All you have to do is bring it to me." He rocked back on his heels, his smile smug. "Piece of cake, and nobody will suspect a thing."

"How long do we have to do this?" She didn't intend to ask that question out loud, but somehow did. "A few days? Weeks?"

"For as long as it takes. You know how Simon Graden is."

She didn't know, and she didn't want to know.

Tommy stared at her a moment. "One more thing. You remember that Agent McLeod from last spring?"

Rachel nodded.

"He's been around town asking questions about you. If I were you, I'd stay away from him."

EIGHT

"What do you mean I'm fired?" Rachel asked the hotel manager, Claudia Smith, a half hour after she left the pool hall.

She had changed out of her skirt and sweater into a pair of jeans and the tunic that made up her uniform. She had taken the cart to the third floor to get started when she'd received a summons to the manager's office. So, here she was, wondering how to defend her job to a sixty-year-old woman with dyed red hair and fingernails long enough to be considered weapons.

"Just that. Like I told you when I hired you, I'm interested in people who want to *work* for their pay. Clearly, you don't." Claudia signed the check in front of her and shoved it across the desk toward Rachel.

"I don't understand."

"You must think I'm stupid," Claudia said with a bitter chuckle. "When you call in that you'll be late because you're taking care of a family crisis, that's a little vague, a little suspicious, but I think to myself okay. But when I see you go into a pool hall when I'm on my way to the bank, I think to myself, 'She's lied to me.'" She caught Rachel's gaze, her eyes hard. "Nobody lies to me and gets away with it."

The accusation stung because it was true, and humiliation made Rachel's lips go numb. Never mind that she'd had a good reason, she thought as she picked up the check and stared at the meager amount she'd earned yesterday.

"That was some sob story about you in the paper last spring," Claudia said, making Rachel turn around. "I kept thinking that if the rumored accusations were true, you'd be in jail like your friend, so I was willing to take a chance to help you out. There's a big difference between helping out and handing out."

"Yes, there is," Rachel said. "And even though I can't tell you why I was at the—" she waved a hand "—you know. I had a very good reason for being there and it won't happen again."

"That's right, it won't," Claudia said. "Because you won't be here."

"I need this job—"

"You should have thought of that before you went gallivanting off to a den of sin instead of coming to work."

"It wasn't like that."

"No, of course it wasn't. Same excuse as my deadbeat husband always had." Fired up now, she continued in a derisive tone. "He had to meet somebody and a bar or pool hall was the only place they could agree on. Or he had a sure business deal, and they had to meet at some strip club." She frowned at Rachel. "You'll be helping yourself out if you stay away from joints like that and spend more time at work and in church instead."

Wanting in the worst way to defend herself, Rachel opened her mouth, then realized there was nothing she could say that would change this woman's mind, especially since anything she said would sound like the husband's excuses. "Thank you for the check."

She closed the door behind her, then stood in the hall, her eyes closed against this latest setback. Why should she be surprised? "I could use a little help here, God," she whispered, the prayer her first in months except for last night's grace.

She had been taught all her life that the end never justified the means. She believed it to the depths of her soul. And this morning, she had gone against those very principles by pretending that she would do something she knew was wrong. And here was the payment for that act.

Rachel got into her car thinking about the conversation that she'd had with Micah on her way here a scant hour ago. He'd given her a cell phone and asked her to check in, which she had done. He'd been both surprised at Tommy's request and grimly pleased that they seemed to be making progress. A plan that depended on her having a job.

Now what? Find another job? She looked down the frontage road that was lined with motels, most of which she had applied to only two days before. The idea of going through the same thing again pressed down on her. At the moment, she couldn't face doing that again.

Once, before gasoline got so expensive, she had

taken rides to clear her head. She could drive toward Aspen and stop at a dozen different places along the bank of the Crystal River where the view would be breathtaking. Or head east on the Interstate and drive into Glenwood Canyon where red, pine-covered cliffs soared hundreds of feet into the air. Or head west on the Interstate where a wide valley stretched on either side of the Colorado River and the vast, forested Grand Mesa rose to the south.

The responsible thing was go find another job, one at a hotel so she could fulfill Graden's awful demand.

A tap on the window of the passenger door scared a year off her life.

She looked over, and Micah stood there. She leaned across the seat and unlocked the door.

He opened it and leaned in. "Are you okay?"

Only then did she realize she had a steady wash of tears down her face. "I was fired."

"Ah, Rachel." He sat down in the passenger seat and closed the door.

"For the second time in three days. And the thing about it is, if an employee had told me the same lame story I had, I would have done the same thing." She glanced over at him. "What are you doing here?"

"Checking on you." He nodded toward the street where cars flowed along at a fairly steady pace. "You haven't met Nico yet, but he's over there in the Denny's parking lot keeping an eye out, and since you've been sitting here in the car for a half hour, he called me."

"I see." She couldn't decide if she was relieved or

upset that she was being watched. In either case, knowing that she had been was weird.

"And you came?" She reached for a tissue in the console and wiped her face, then blew her nose. Stupid question since he was here.

"As soon as he called me," Micah said.

Those simple words warmed her, though she was pretty sure they shouldn't.

"I think you need a break," he said. "Lock up your car, and let's take mine." He opened the door and got out.

When she didn't immediately open the door, he tapped on the roof of the car. "Come on. I bet you didn't have any lunch, either."

That was true, but she hadn't been eating lunch in months.

She got out of the car and locked it.

"Good, you're wearing jeans and walking shoes. I didn't make it to Hanging Lake last spring and today is definitely a playing hooky kind of day." He led the way to his vehicle and opened the door for her, waiting for her to climb in before going to the driver's side. When he got in and started the engine, he said, "Personally I'm starved for a burger and a malt. What about you?"

She was still stuck on the idea of Micah playing hooky, not to mention hiking to one of her favorite places. "And you want to hike after eating that?"

Grinning, he nodded.

She glanced at her watch. "Twenty minutes to eat, fifteen minutes to drive to the trail head, and a four-hour hike." She shook her head. "Tempted as I am to go along with this madness, we can't get back before my kids will be home from school."

Micah's grin grew wider. "Pull the other leg, Rachel. I know your dad is taking care of the kids today. You have all afternoon."

"But—"

He pressed a finger against her lips. "Be spontaneous. I'll send Nico and Erin to keep an eye on your family. You need a break and I want to do this for you."

"Hanging Lake is one of my favorite places," she conceded.

He put the vehicle into gear. "I remember that."

Her thoughts turned back to when they had first met each other last spring. They'd talked about a lot of things—always her talking about her life—but she didn't remember telling him about Hanging Lake.

Before leaving the parking lot, Micah called Erin and Nico, letting them know where they were headed and giving them instructions to watch over Rachel's family. With everything going on, taking time away to simply relax was an unaffordable luxury. The stress Rachel was under, though, had to be broken somehow. A few hours away from it all was the best he could manage today.

Assured her family was being looked after to the best of his ability, Micah went through a drive-through, and then they headed east on Interstate 70.

The aroma of French fries filled the vehicle, and Rachel opened the sack and pulled a couple of fries out, then blushed when he looked at her. Her embarrassment didn't keep her from nibbling on one, though, which made him laugh.

She smiled back, and a nameless something eased in his chest. He was doing the right thing by taking her away for a couple of hours.

Within minutes, the smooth ribbon of highway entered the canyon, winding along with the Colorado River and the railway bed. While they ate lunch at a picnic table at the rest stop that marked the trailhead that led to Hanging Lake, Micah deliberately kept the conversation to the most mundane things he could think of. The weather—which was one of those gorgeous September days with a brilliant blue sky—and the engineering feat the highway through the narrow canyon represented. And he kept thinking about how much he wanted her to know him—Micah, the man, not the special agent.

And he felt as tongue-tied as he had when he was a sixteen-year-old more comfortable talking to horses than to girls.

"Ready?" he asked, after gathering up their trash and throwing it in a nearby receptacle.

"No, but since we're here…" A small smile took away the negative answer.

"No?" he teased.

She headed up the paved pathway where a sign pointed the way. "That's because I've been here and I know how strenuous this is. It's straight up. We climb almost a thousand feet in a bit over a mile."

Micah glanced back at the river. "Maybe we should have gone fishing instead."

"You'll miss one of the prettiest places you'll ever see, then."

He caught up with her, the enthusiasm in her voice so alluring he wanted more of it.

A short distance later, they left the paved bicycle path that continued along the river shore and headed up a rocky trail.

And, she was right. The trail went up steeply and by a hundred yards in, Micah wondered how he was going to manage a full mile of this. Ahead of him, Rachel was walking at her own pace, moving steadily without stopping at any of the benches strategically located along the trail.

Within a quarter mile, they had climbed more than a hundred feet from the canyon bottom, and the sound of the river faded.

"Are you doing okay back there?" she called to him.

No tension in her voice, which pleased him to no end. "Great."

He ran wind sprints all the time and kept up a fitness regimen that kept him in great shape. Or so he had believed until the last fifteen minutes. He hoped she wouldn't notice that his answer was more of a gasp than a shout.

"We can stop if you want to rest," she said.

"Nope," he lied. "I'm fine." By now his focus had narrowed to putting one foot in front of the other, and he didn't notice that she had stopped until her planted feet—facing him, no less—came into view. He looked up and found her smiling.

Not the guarded smile she'd had earlier, but a

genuine, delighted smile. He decided being out of breath and feeling as though his lungs might explode was worth it. She extended a bottle of water toward him.

"I think you've been spending too much time doing paperwork and not enough time chasing bad guys," she teased.

He took the bottle from her. "Maybe."

"I doubt it," she said, her voice more serious. "It's just the straight up climb combined with the altitude."

"Let's hope you're right. Otherwise, I'll never pass my next DEA physical." As he unscrewed the cap and took a drink, he glanced back at where they had come from. The deep red earth that gave the Colorado its name was vivid against the rich green of the pines and the blue sky overhead.

"Do you really have a ranch?" she asked, the question bringing his focus back to her.

"I really do." He tipped back the brim of his Stetson so he could see her face.

She seemed to ponder that answer for a moment before smiling again. "Evidently without any big mountains like this one."

"Not this big," he agreed, "but some real pretty country and a view of the Tetons from the front porch of my house."

She gave him another thoughtful look before turning back toward the steep trail in front of them. "The steepest part of the trail is ahead of us."

"Let's go," he said.

They hadn't been walking long before they encountered a group of hikers on their way down, exclaiming at how gorgeous the views were. Since only thin metal handrails provided a safety hold against a hundred foot drop, he was thankful he wasn't squeamish about heights. After climbing up a set of steps cut into the rock, they approached a more level area.

Ferns and moss-covered rocks lined the narrow, shallow stream whose high-water mark indicated it sometimes ran many feet higher. Golden-leafed cotton-woods provided welcome shade overhead. All of it was lush, soothing to the senses, and worth every agonizing step to get here.

Ahead, the cliff walls widened outwards, and there was the lake, pristine and even more beautiful than he had imagined. Ahead of him, Rachel found a seat along the boardwalk surrounding the lake's edge. Catching his breath, he joined her.

"This is worth every single stitch in my side," he said, sitting down next to her and setting his hat underneath the bench. "What's with the boardwalk?"

"The Boy Scouts built it to protect the fragile shore-line from eroding away under the onslaught of all the hikers."

Micah imagined what the construction must have been like since the building materials would have been hauled up the trail they had just taken.

"I haven't been up here in a couple of years." Her attention remained focused on the water in front of them. "And I should have come. I'd forgotten how rejuvenating this place is."

A few other hikers were on the other side of the lake, closer to a white veil of a waterfall that fell into transparent, emerald-green water. In the shallows in front of them, trout, no more than two or three inches long, swam.

He glanced at Rachel, whose eyes were closed and her head tilted back as though she was listening to the gentle lap of the water and the chirp of birds, punctuated now and then with the raucous call of a blue jay.

"When I was a kid," she said, bending over to pick up a small stone, polishing it against her jeans, "I always found God in places like this more than in church. And since my dad was a minister, I always felt guilty about that."

"If God's not here, I don't know where He'd be," Micah said. "This looks like Eden to me."

She nodded. "It does, doesn't it?" After a few minutes of comfortable silence, she added, "I wasn't sure anything you told me last spring was the truth."

There wasn't a single thing he could say to defend that, so he remained silent.

She turned her head toward him. "I'm glad you have a ranch. It's reassuring to know something was real."

"Except for my cover and the things directly related to the investigation," he said, "it was all real. Sticking to the truth as much as you can makes the job easier. In your case…" He sighed. "In your case, I wanted to be completely truthful with you."

She looked away, and once more the silence stretched between them, not quite as comfortable as it was before. Then, her voice so low that he had to bend close to hear her, she said, "I had been so sure we were friends…"

He took her hand, clasping her palm against his. "We were, Rachel. That was as real as it got, and I died a little each day knowing that I couldn't tell you who I really was."

"I still don't know. You do this job." She waved her free hand, which still held the smooth stone. "And yet you have a ranch, and I remember last spring you spoke of it with so much love that I couldn't imagine how you could leave it."

"My dad and mother take care of it, and my salary supports it. For a small operation like ours, the margins are too slim to keep it going without an outside income." He paused a moment, needing to tell her the rest of it and not at all sure that she would understand. "Plus, I like my job."

She looked at him then, her hand still within his, her fingers clasping him back. "You do? How could you?"

Since her tone was curious rather than judging, he wanted to tell her. Still, putting into words what he'd never told anyone wasn't so easy. "My best friend in college—"

"Brady?"

"Yes. Did I tell you this story?"

"You mentioned he was a friend who had died of a drug overdose."

Micah held her gaze while he processed that he had no recollection of telling her about his friend. Yet he'd been so sure he had remembered every exchange between them.

"The official report says that he committed suicide, and technically he did. I never believed it, though, because he was trying to get clean, and he was doing out-patient rehab. I always believed his supplier wanted to make sure he couldn't talk. What better way to shut him up than to give the man a huge dose of LSD."

"He died," she murmured, her gaze once more focused on the lake in front of them as she reassuringly squeezed his hand. "And you found a calling."

"That's right."

"I used to think I knew what mine was." She pulled her hand from his, continuing to rub the stone. "Lately, at every turn, a new obstacle crops up, and I'm back at square one."

"I've been there, too." Was there right now, if he were honest with himself. Their relationship had been filled with obstacles from the beginning. He wanted more. He hoped today, right now, was a foundation for more. "Your dad reminded me yesterday that prayer is the first step."

"Yeah, well, that's my dad's thing."

"Not yours?"

Looking away, she shook her head. "No, not mine. God and I aren't speaking right now."

Her softly spoken, matter-of-fact words punched him in the middle of his chest and left him breathless. One of the many things he'd been drawn to in her was her deep reservoir of faith. She'd been enthusiastic and joyful when he'd first met her, her expression often reflecting her satisfaction with life instead of the sadness etched there now. She'd been a woman of faith, and that was one of many things he loved about her.

This was one more thing he owed her. "My fault," he said.

She glanced at him. "Much as I'd like to blame somebody for my loss of faith, I can't. Not even you."

"Besides the obvious, what happened?" He turned slightly to face her, his attention completely on her. "You would have been at the top of my list of people least likely to lose it."

She shrugged, her gaze falling to the stone she worried between her fingers. "It's a little hard to keep having faith when everything in your life disintegrates. I kept praying for God to get me out of this mess, and things just keep getting worse."

He took both of her hands within his, capturing the stone. "The Bible is full of prayers like that. Like the verse from one of the Psalms that goes something like 'Why, God, have You turned away from me?' or like poor old Job bemoaning the day he was born."

"Yes," she whispered. "Exactly like that."

"Is your life really so bad as that, Rachel?" Regret clogged his voice, regret that he hadn't done more to ease the way for her. Since he'd admitted to himself that he loved her, how could he have let it get to this point? He picked up the smooth stone, warm from her holding it. "What about Sarah and Andy? What about this beautiful place?"

When she looked at him, he bent his head toward her until his forehead rested against hers. "I believe that prayer doesn't change God, but rather the person praying. And, I believe the first step to that is seeing the possibility for things to get better." When she turned her head and looked away, he asked, "What would you be doing, Rachel, if you really believed you were defeated? I mean really defeated, where things are as bad as they could get."

"I don't know what you mean."

"If you didn't have hope, wouldn't you have stopped doing everything to take care of yourself and your children?"

"I couldn't do that."

"I know. That's the point." He handed the stone back to her. "There's that verse from Mark where Jesus talks about the clean and the unclean. I know the context had to do with the disciples eating with dirty hands and the keeping of old traditions, but I've always thought that what He said about what comes out of your heart being unclean made so much sense. My take on it was that I have a choice to have good intentions in my heart or evil ones, and I'd be clean or unclean as a result."

Rachel remembered the verse, and she felt as though Micah had flicked on a light that illuminated the dark corners of her heart. She'd stopped noticing the good in her life, and she'd stopped being thankful. The worry and fear that consumed her were a result, she thought. Not a cause. He was right. She *did* have a lot to be thankful for, and she'd stopped noticing. Maybe she couldn't change her circumstances—yet—but she could throw away her fear and her worry, and act as if it were already done, just the way she had been taught all her life.

With that, she threw the stone as far into the lake as she could, then picked up another and threw it.

Micah threw one, too, asking, "What are we doing?"

She laughed. "Throwing away the stones that weigh me down."

NINE

"You're up," Erin Asher said the following morning as Rachel came into the kitchen. "I thought you might sleep in since you didn't have a job to go to this morning." She was sitting at the kitchen table, the morning paper and a yogurt container in front of her.

Tightening the sash to her velour robe around her waist, Rachel responded, "Old habits and all that." Pouring a cup of coffee, she looked out the window to her favorite time of day—those moments just before and after sunrise. The mountains to the east of town were a silhouette against the pale gray sky. She added cream to her coffee and took the first sip. Out of habit she tested the soil of the plants set on the sill above the sink. "Did you sleep okay?"

"Fine." Erin grinned. "That bed is very comfortable. Far better than any hotel I've stayed in lately."

"Good." Yesterday afternoon after Rachel and Micah had returned from their hike, he'd suggested that Erin move in with them for the duration. Since she had plenty of room, that made sense to Rachel. Last night, she'd felt a sense of relief that Erin was in the house, and she'd had her best night's sleep in weeks.

"Micah and I talked a little while ago," Erin said. "Instead of you looking for another maid's job at yet another hotel, we think a better plan is to hold out and see what Graden's next move is."

"You've already spoken with Micah this morning?" He must be an even earlier riser than she was, since it was just past five-thirty.

Erin grinned. "Twice. He's determined to make sure all the bases are covered."

Rachel took another sip of her coffee, remembering how dismissive Tommy had been when she'd called him last night to let him know that she had been fired and so she wouldn't be working this morning. Mostly, she was relieved she wouldn't have to be on the lookout for some illicit package that she wanted nothing to do with. "The only problem is, I need the job."

She worked weekends as a waitress at Shepherd's Inn where the hourly wage was low but the tips were good. Her third job was restoring and refinishing old furniture, which she loved, but it didn't pay until the job was finished.

"Micah said to tell you not to worry about that. He'd make sure whatever shortfall you have is covered."

"Getting Graden is so important that my salary will be covered?" Not that her salary came close to covering her "shortfall," but Erin didn't need to know that.

"I don't know about all that—you'll have to talk to Micah."

Rachel intended to. Though one part of her was

relieved, at another level, she didn't like it. Her gaze strayed to the clock on the stove. Not going to work this morning meant that she had more time on her hands than she'd had in months. Oddly enough, she couldn't decide what she even thought about it. The free hours she'd had yesterday afternoon had been a gift she hadn't expected to have again so soon.

She emptied the grounds from the coffeemaker, and discovering the wastebasket full, pulled out the plastic liner, which she carried to the door.

"I'll be back in a minute," she said to Erin, stepping outside.

The air was chilly, though quite a few degrees away from the first frost of the season. It was quiet except for the chirping of a robin who seemed to be announcing the sun would rise soon. Rachel soaked in the crisp feel and scent of the air, her moments of calm before it was time to get the kids up and rush headlong into the day.

Once, she had spent this time praying. Once. She swallowed, admitting she wasn't quite ready for that even as she made a point of cataloging the things she was thankful for, beginning with Micah and his team watching over her children. This morning, she felt safe, and she hadn't in a long time.

Stepping off the back stoop, she headed down the walkway to the rear of the garage and the fence that separated the yard from the alley where the garbage cans were kept. The yard was bathed in varying shades of gray except for the vivid hues of the bright yellow marigolds planted along the back fence.

Just as she opened the gate, she thought she smelled

paint. Something clattered to the ground. She stepped into the alley and came face-to-face with a guy holding a can of spray paint.

He swore.

"What are you doing?" she demanded, taking in words on the garage door and that he was a gangly kid no taller than herself and not old enough to be shaving yet.

He aimed the spray can at her, and she threw the bag of trash at him. It exploded and spewed garbage everywhere.

He turned and ran toward a bike leaned against the garage.

She ran after him, incensed now. "Come back here!"

He ran with the bike, leaping on it like a cowboy making a running mount on his horse. And she knew she wouldn't be able to catch him. "You come back here, you coward."

"Rachel?" Erin called from the back of the house.

"Back here." Rachel watched the kid speed away, disgusted that she hadn't been able to stop him. Her attention turned then to the mess on the ground and the graffiti on the garage doors.

Impressions pelted her like dozens of sharp pebbles. Vile words. Filthy words. This was no random tagging by a gang member. The words used her name, calling her a drug dealer and worse. Nasty words no kid should know sprayed on the doors in white, the paint so thick that it had run.

Raw, violent anger churned through her at the violation of having her property defaced like this. Restoring the 1920s-era doors and painting them the same park-bench green as the shutters on the house had been a huge undertaking two years ago, a task to keep her from dwelling on her husband's death. What would her neighbors think when they saw this? How could she explain this to anyone? Though the hateful words were a lie, she felt shamed by them.

At the end of the block, the kid turned the corner and disappeared from view.

She began to shake.

Erin came through the gate. "What in the world?" When her gaze lit on the garage doors, she pulled her cell phone from her pocket, pushed a single button to make a call, and a second later said, "You need to get here right now. We're in the alley behind the house."

Rachel pulled the lid off the trash barrel and began picking up the contents of the bag, mostly to give herself something to do, mostly to keep from screaming her frustration at this latest insult. "That was Micah you called?"

"Yes," Erin said. "Don't touch the cans of paint."

"I won't." She hadn't noticed them until that instant. One looked as though it hadn't been opened, the other had been dropped by the kid when he had run away.

"Are you okay?"

A simple question. She should have been able respond without her voice quivering.

A second later she heard running footsteps along the walkway next to the garage, and Micah pushed open the gate. His encompassing gaze took it all in before landing on her.

"Are you hurt?" When she shook her head, he added, "What were you doing out here?"

"I was bringing out the trash from the kitchen, and I caught him."

His eyes sharpened. "What do you mean you caught him?"

"Red-handed, in the act," Rachel said, relating what had happened.

"What did he look like?" Micah opened his cell phone and punched a number.

"A kid. My height, I guess, maybe a tiny bit taller. He isn't shaving yet."

Someone evidently answered Micah's call because he said, "I know it's been a short night, but I need you here now." Closing the phone, he looked at Erin. "Head out to the end of the alley and see if he left anything behind. I'm going to circle around the opposite direction. I'll meet you on Main."

Erin took off at a fast walk, her attention mostly on the graveled track of the alley.

Micah looked back at Rachel. "I want you to go into the house and call the police. And I want you to stay there until Nico gets here."

"But—"

"No buts, Rachel." His implacable tone matched his expression as he opened the gate and turned her toward it. "You need to be inside with the children."

She searched his eyes, thinking about all the unsaid things conveyed in that simple statement. "Okay."

The instant she was inside the gate, she heard him stride away.

All at once bereft, she looked around the yard where it was now light enough that colors were more apparent than they had been a few minutes ago. The eastern sky had turned to cream, and she knew the sun would be up in a few more minutes.

Inside, she dialed the police, reporting the graffiti and her confrontation. The dispatcher told her that an officer would be by within the hour.

"Who were you calling?" Sarah asked from the kitchen doorway, her hair mussed and her well-loved teddy bear under one arm.

"Good morning, my love." Rachel held out her arms, sitting down on one of the kitchen chairs.

Sarah perched on her lap, her bunny slippers peeking out from the hem of her nightgown. "You're not dressed, Mom."

"No, not yet." Rachel glanced down at her long velour robe and slippers with some surprise. She had intended to get a cup of coffee and take her shower. Instead, she'd confronted a vandal. A vandal who worked for Simon Graden, either directly or indirectly. She was sure of it.

"You're gonna be late for work."

Rachel glanced outside where the first rays of sunlight were peeking over the mountain. "No work this morning. Instead, I can hang out with you until it's time to go to school."

"I'd like it if you could stay home all the time like Amelia's mom."

"Here it comes," Rachel said lightly, "the daily guilt trip."

"Mom."

Rachel pressed a kiss against her daughter's head.

"You know that working is part of the deal. Why don't you get your brother up while I go get dressed."

Sarah jumped off her lap. "And then we can have awful waffles?"

"Sure," Rachel responded with a grin. Her children might call toaster waffles awful, but they were still a favorite though a distant second to homemade.

Sarah ran up the stairs ahead of her, calling Andy's name and barging into his room. In response, he yelled at her to leave him alone. And, Rachel found herself smiling. Her children, following their normal routine. Normal.

Her smile faded, and she reached for the phone on the wall. Dialing the number on Simon Graden's card, which she'd tacked to the cork board, she counted off the rings while her palms became increasingly sweaty.

"Good morning, Rachel," came his smooth voice after the third ring.

She was so startled that he'd called her by name, she didn't say anything for a moment. He probably had caller ID.

"I hope you're calling to tell me that you've found the item I'm looking for."

Tired of the coy game, she said, "I don't have your money, Mr. Graden. I never had it. I don't know where it is, but I can tell you one thing. I've had enough. I came face-to-face with your thug this morning, and I'm done. Leave me alone. Leave my children and my father alone. The police are on the way here, and I'm telling them—"

"What?" he interrupted. "That you called me at daybreak to complain about some misfortune you're having? I have no idea what you're talking about."

"You won't get away with this," Rachel said. "You or your thugs come near my house again, and I'll be forced to take matters into my own hands."

"And that sounds quite like a threat that should be reported." The line went dead then.

Rachel pulled the receiver away from her ear and stared at it. Of all the stupid things she might have done, this topped the list.

She had just finished dressing when the doorbell rang. Nico stood on the porch. He was at least a decade younger than Micah, and last night Rachel had learned that he sometimes posed as a teenager while working undercover.

"Is Micah back yet?" he asked when she opened the door.

"Not yet." She stood to the side so he could come in. Beyond his shoulder, she watched a police cruiser come to a stop in front of the house. She hoped this offense would be taken more seriously than the last one she had called in. Then, they had attributed the rock thrown through her window to pranksters, and she had wanted to think so, too.

When Nico saw the officer get out of the car, he asked, "Okay if I hang around while you talk to him?"

Rachel had assumed he'd want to, so the question puzzled her a little.

"As a family friend," he tacked on.

"Sure." She understood he was encouraging her not to tell the officer he was a DEA agent, but she didn't understand why. She opened the door as the police officer came up the walkway. "Please come in."

"Thanks, ma'am. I understand you had some trouble with vandals this morning."

"I did." With that, Rachel led the way to the alley. Now that the sun was up and shining directly on the doors, the words were even more obscene than they'd seemed when she first read them.

"I think a pressure washer will probably get the worst of this off," Nico said, as if understanding the direction of her thoughts.

Throughout taking the report, the officer was polite, vacillating between this being a prank by the teenage boy she had confronted and being the result of her making someone angry.

"Anyone mad at you about anything?" the officer asked. "Anyone holding a grudge for some reason?"

"No one has any reason to hold a grudge," she said, resisting the urge to clap her hand over her mouth. It was the truth. Just not the whole truth.

The officer bagged the two cans of paint and neatly labeled them after taking pictures of the door. He gave her his card with the case number on it and told her they'd let her know if they found the perpetrator. As they headed back toward the house, he warned her that any fingerprints they might find on the can might not be traceable.

Rachel followed the officer back to the front door as the kids came running down the stairs.

"What was that policeman doing here?" Andy asked while Sarah said, "Mom, Andy was pulling my hair and he won't give me my hairbrush." When her gaze lit on Nico, she added, "Mr. Nico, you're back. Are you going to have waffles with us?"

"Well, I dunno. That depends on your mother, I guess."

"Mom," Andy interrupted, moving to stand in front of her, his arms crossed and Sarah's hairbrush in one hand. "What about that policeman?"

"He's going to arrest you for stealing my brush," Sarah said.

Rachel took the hairbrush from him and handed it to Sarah. "He was just checking on a kid who was hanging around here this morning." That was the truth, simply not the whole truth. Rachel had a sudden appreciation for the way Micah often weighed what he was going to say. The trick was to keep to the truth, or at least as much as you could manage in the moment. Another realization to put into the hopper and mull over, especially since she had turned into a bold-faced liar not ten minutes ago. She caught Nico's glance. "And yes, you're more than welcome to have breakfast with us."

"Come on," Sarah said, taking him by the hand. "Since you're tall, you can get them out of the freezer."

"Them?" Nico questioned, allowing himself to be led.

"Waffles."

"That sounds good," Nico said.

Rachel turned back to close the front door and saw that Micah and Erin were halfway up the block.

"Did you find him?" Rachel asked after they came through the front door.

"No," Erin said, heading down the hallway toward the kitchen.

"I'm sorry," Micah said.

"For not catching him?" The kid had been peddling as fast as he could the last she saw him. "He was long gone."

"This shouldn't have happened on my watch."

That sounded to Rachel like he'd taken the vandalism personally. "Does that mean what I think it does— that you kept watch over the house last night?"

"Part of it. Nico and I took turns."

She studied him a moment, having no idea what to say about that. She could imagine how he felt—that he'd done his best, and it hadn't been enough. Since she now had her own secrets to keep—no way did she want to confess that she had called Graden—there wasn't a lot she could say.

While they all ate breakfast, her children were happy, showing off for their company and reveling in all the extra attention, especially Micah's. Their silliness had him smiling even though the expression didn't quite reach his eyes. Nico and Erin fitted right in, as well, and Rachel admitted that she liked having the company.

They went over the schedule for the day, which included Rachel's Friday evening job as a waitress at Shepherd's Inn.

Erin went with her when she drove the kids to school. She was watchful, and Rachel found herself being so, as well. The vandal this morning had been only a kid. Would she recognize him if she came face to face with him again? She doubted she would.

At the school, the kids ran in, and Rachel remained where she was, watching them until they were safely

A SERIES OF EDGE-OF-YOUR-SEAT SUSPENSE NOVELS!

GET 2 FREE BOOKS!

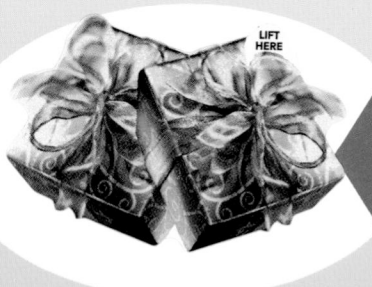

LIFT HERE

To get your 2 free books, affix this peel-off sticker to the reply card and mail it today!

Plus, receive
TWO FREE BONUS GIFTS!

Love Inspired®
SUSPENSE
RIVETING INSPIRATIONAL ROMANCE

We'd like to send you two free books to introduce you to the Love Inspired® Suspense series. Your two books have a combined c price of $9.98 in the U.S. and $11.98 in Canada, but they are yours We'll even send you two wonderful surprise gifts. You can't lose!

married to the mob
GINNY AIKEN

Double Deception
Terri Reed

VALERIE HANSEN
Out of the Depths

SHIRLEE McCOY
Little Girl Lost
THE SECRETS OF STONELEY

LOIS RICHER
IDENTITY: UNDERCOVER
FINDERS...INC

Each of your **FREE** books is filled with riveting inspirational suspense featuring Christian characters facing challenges to t faith...and their lives!

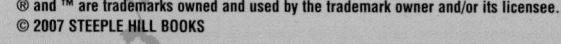

GET 2 FREE BOOKS!

HURRY!
Return this card promptly to get 2 FREE Books and 2 FREE Bonus Gifts!

YES! Please send me the **2 FREE Love Inspired® Suspense books** and **2 FREE gifts** for which I qualify. I understand that I am under no obligation to purchase anything further, as explained on the back of this card.

Love Inspired
SUSPENSE
RIVETING INSPIRATIONAL ROMANCE

PLACE FREE GIFTS SEAL HERE

▼ DETACH AND MAIL CARD TODAY! ▼

LISUS-IV-07

323 IDL EL5D   123 IDL EL4D

FIRST NAME	LAST NAME

ADDRESS

APT.#	CITY

STATE/PROV.	ZIP/POSTAL CODE

If offer card is missing write to:

Steeple Hill Reader Service, 3010 Walden Ave., P.O. Box 1867, Buffalo, NY 14240-1867

Steeple Hill Reader Service™ — Here's How It Works:

Accepting your 2 free books and 2 free gifts places you under no obligation to buy anything. You may keep the books and gifts and return the shipping statement marked "cancel." If you do not cancel, about a month later we'll send you 4 additional books and bill you just $3.99 each in the U.S. or $4.74 each in Canada, plus 25¢ shipping & handling per book and applicable taxes if any.* That's the complete price and — compared to cover prices of $4.99 each in the U.S. and $5.99 each in Canada — it's quite a bargain! You may cancel at any time, but if you choose to continue, every month we'll send you 4 more books, which you may either purchase at the discount price or return to us and cancel your subscription.

*Terms and prices subject to change without notice. Sales tax applicable in N.Y. Canadian residents will be charged applicable provincial taxes and GST. All orders subject to approval. Books received may vary. Credit or debit balances in a customer's account(s) may be offset by any other outstanding balance owed by or to the customer. Please allow 4 to 6 weeks for delivery.

inside. When they got back to the house, Micah and Nico had put together a list of components needed to add cameras at the alley and back door, their planning so deliberate it gave Rachel chills.

Nico and Erin left to get the supplies, and Rachel was left with Micah.

"I keep thinking about two different things," she said. "First, Tommy Manderoll warned me to stay away from you."

"That's not surprising since I went to see him when I first got to town."

"You haven't exactly been hiding when you've come here, so he could know—Graden could know that you're here."

"I didn't expect this to be a covert operation this time," Micah said. "But I also haven't seen any indication that anyone is watching you." He managed a smile. "Of course, I'm the same guy who let a punk get close enough to paint graffiti on the garage. What's the other thing on your mind?"

"I want to go back to my store. Do a search there for Graden's money. Can you get in?"

He nodded. "I don't think anything is there, Rachel. The place was cleaned out."

"I know, but it's an old building with a few nooks and crannies that could have been overlooked."

"Going there is going to be depressing," he warned.

Hours later, Rachel had no choice but to agree with him. It *had* been depressing. The building had been empty, just as it had been when she and Angela were first looking for a store. But instead of being filled with hope and possibilities and anticipation as it had been then, all that was left were bittersweet memories. And no sign of Graden's money anywhere.

After she picked Andy up from kindergarten, the afternoon sped by. Since it was the first day she had been able to spend mostly at home in a long time, Rachel found herself wishing the clock would slow just a little. While Erin and Micah were working on something in the den, she helped Nico powerwash the doors to the garage. As he had promised, the spray paint came off, and the doors didn't look any worse for the wear.

When it was time to pick up Sarah from school, she went to Andy's room to ask if he wanted to go with her. He wasn't there, which wasn't a huge surprise since the day outside was a beautiful one. He and his friend Jeremy had been in and out of the house so many times, she had finally told the boys to choose in or out and stay there for a while. Since they weren't in Andy's room, they were undoubtedly outside, probably at the small jumping ramp Jeremy's father had built for them.

Except, the boys weren't there, nor in the backyard at the swing set, nor in the sand with the dump trucks.

"Have you seen Andy?" she asked, coming back through the house and into the den where Erin and Micah were working.

"I heard them run through just a couple of minutes ago," Erin said.

Rachel headed for the kitchen to call Jeremy's mother.

"I thought they were at your house," she told Rachel. "I looked out maybe fifteen minutes ago, and the two of them were riding up and down the sidewalk in front of your place."

"I'll go check again," Rachel said, forcing herself to breathe.

"And I'll do the same on this end of the block. Maybe they went to the McCurdy's house. I saw him tinkering in his workshop earlier."

Hoping Jeremy's mother was right, Rachel hung up the phone and went to the front of the house, looking up and down the street for her son and his friend.

No bicycles.

No boys.

TEN

"Breathe," Micah said. He urged Rachel out of the door and toward the wicker chair on the porch. He'd heard enough to know that Andy was missing. Easy as it was to jump to the worst conclusions, chances were good the boy was close by and fine.

"I can't just sit down," Rachel said around a gulping breath. "I've got to find him. And Jeremy, too."

Nico and Erin followed them onto the porch.

"What has it been? Ten minutes since you last saw Andy?" Micah asked.

Rachel jerked her head once.

Micah looked from Erin to Nico. "You two know what to do. Check in every ten minutes."

They headed down the walk and got into the vehicle that Nico had arrived in earlier.

Rachel looked shell-shocked. He gently urged her into the chair.

"Where else would he go?"

She bent her head and pressed her fingers to her eyes. "I don't know. Maybe to the alley since we were back there this morning and he was so curious about the policeman. Maybe… He knows he can't leave the block and that he's to stay in sight of the house."

"Then, let's go check the alley." When she didn't immediately fall into step beside him, he looked back at her. "We'll find him, Rachel. I promise."

She stood, her expression fierce. "Don't make promises you might not be able to keep." She sucked in a shuddering breath and pressed a hand against her chest. "This is my fault."

Still heading toward the back of the house, he shook his head. "He's just being a kid. It's nobody's fault. He'll turn up."

"No. You don't understand. It's Graden—"

"It's probably not," Micah said, doing his best to sound reassuring, the familiar knot in the middle of his chest tightening at the sound of the man's name.

"Because I called him." Her voice trailed off miserably, and when Micah turned around to look at her she added, "This morning."

He was positive he must have misunderstood her.

"I told him to leave us alone and that I was sick of the games and—" She stretched out a hand, her voice so choked he could barely understand her. "I threatened him."

The words made about as much sense to Micah as they would have if she'd told him she'd murdered someone or had shaved her head. Her threatening anyone, even Graden, simply didn't compute.

"What if he's taken my son?" Tears welled in her eyes.

"Let's keep looking before we jump to any conclusions." He didn't dare follow her line of reasoning or he'd be as panicked as she was. Torn between the need to see if Andy was in the alley and to comfort Rachel, he settled with taking her hand and pulling her along with him as they headed toward the back fence. "Tell me what happened."

She related the conversation. While calling Graden definitely wasn't a smart move, her "I'll be forced to take matters into my own hands" wasn't the kind of threat that would get her in any trouble unless the man showed up dead and there was a direct link to Rachel. He could imagine her being as fierce as a mama bear to protect her children. Otherwise, the idea of Rachel hurting anyone was inconceivable.

Every bit of logic dictated that Andy was in the neighborhood. Micah hadn't wanted to scare the kids with any doomsday talk, and so the best choice had been to let them be kids. Once more, though, he was fast realizing this wasn't the kind of operation he was prepared for. A kid wasn't supposed to disappear in the space of five minutes when he had been playing in front of his own house.

The alley was empty of people, most especially small boys on bicycles. The ground in front of the garage was wet, a leftover from the power spray used to wash the graffiti from the garage doors. Micah noticed bicycle tracks, which could have been Andy or one of the other kids in the neighborhood.

"Could he have gone to your dad's house?" Micah asked.

"I hope not," she responded. "I'll call him, though."

Micah mentally traveled the route between Rachel's house and her father's. Part of the trip was along a busy strip of road without any sidewalks. Definitely not the place for a five-year-old.

He followed her to the house and impatiently listened while she and her father talked. The gist was that Andy wasn't there and her dad would head in this direction to see if he was somewhere in between. While she was on the phone, Erin and Nico checked in. They hadn't spotted him, either.

Blaming himself for Andy's disappearance, Micah left the house, telling Rachel that he'd circle the block.

As Rachel hung up the phone, regret swamped her. She should have never, never called Graden. Defacing her property was one thing. The thought of him having her son chilled her until she was shaking. He had been threatening them ever since he had given her the picture. How could she have forgotten that? Her head throbbed with the cadence of her thoughts. She should have taken the children and run.

More rattled by the moment, Rachel headed back outside. Seeing Micah knocking on a door a few houses away, she turned in the opposite direction. Most of her neighbors weren't home, but she knocked on every door, hoping the boys would be there. By the time Rachel reached the end of their street, she was certain that Graden had her son. No other possibility made sense to her.

Her father arrived, and her heart sank even more when she saw that Andy and Jeremy weren't with him. He parked his car in her driveway.

And then, movement at the corner snagged her attention, and her daughter came toward her. Rachel looked down at her watch, realizing school had let out an hour ago. And in her panic about Andy, she hadn't gone to pick up Sarah.

Sarah, who had been alone and unprotected all this time. Rachel's imagination took off at a gallop, and the idea of what she might have lost swamped her.

She bowed her head, then looked up.

Behind Sarah, walking their bicycles, were Andy and Jeremy.

Rachel ran toward them.

"Mom," complained Sarah the instant Rachel was within earshot, "you forgot to pick me up. And Andy got to have ice cream. Why didn't you make him wait until I could go, too?"

"'Cause it was just for guys," Andy said. His face was smeared with what appeared to be the remains of chocolate, his favorite. "And it was really good." He grinned then. "Thanks, Mom."

"I want ice cream, too," Sarah whined.

"Don't you give me that, Andrew Chester Neesham. You know you didn't ask if you could go anywhere," Rachel said to Andy, her relief that he was okay dissolving into anger than he'd left their block without permission. "And just how did you pay for your ice cream?"

"With the money that man gave us," Jeremy offered.

"What man?" Rachel demanded, her heart once again pounding.

"Smitty. You know," Andy said with absolute conviction. "The guy who used to be around your store all the time. The one who smells like peppermints."

"Smitty Jones?" Rachel stared at her son. Smitty, the handyman who had worked for her for years, always had peppermints for the kids when they came into the store. But she hadn't seen him since it closed.

"That's who I told you, Mom," Andy said. "He said that it was okay. You told him it was, and we could go to the malt shop."

"I didn't," Rachel said.

"And I remember that other time," Andy continued, looking earnestly at her, "when we went with him for ice cream. 'Member, Mom?"

"That's besides the point," she said.

"And we did just like he told us," Andy continued without taking a breath. "Eat your ice cream and go home. Don't dawdle. And we didn't, Mom. Honest."

Trembling now, Rachel stepped in front of her son and knelt there. "Sweetie, I haven't talked to Smitty today." In actual fact, she hadn't spoken with him in months. "Don't you remember our talk about not going anywhere with strangers?"

"He wasn't a stranger, Mom. He was Smitty. And besides, he was with that other man who helped Grandpa plant the tree. You remember that, don't you?"

Rachel nodded, flooded with the memory of Graden predicting just this very thing. But this was even worse than she had imagined. He'd somehow used a trusted friend to lure her son away.

As if he had some idea of how upset she was, Andy patted her hand. "It's okay, Mom. We didn't ride our bikes in the street or anything, and we looked both ways at the traffic light, and we didn't talk to any strangers."

"And how did you get there?"

"In the man's pickup."

She heard the last through a roaring in her ears as Sarah said, "Hi Micah. Hi, Mrs. Simpson."

She looked over her shoulder, her gaze falling on Micah and Jeremy's mother. He extended his hand to her. She took it, and he pulled her up, squeezing her hand briefly before letting go.

"Here you guys are," he said, his voice echoing the relief that Rachel felt. "We've been looking everywhere for you."

"We didn't know you were," Jeremy said, his attention mostly on his mother.

"And now it's time to go home," she said, "where you can stay the rest of the day since you left without permission."

His shoulders drooped as he said, "'Bye, Andy," and followed his mother.

"I want to go get ice cream, too," Sarah repeated.

"Not today." Rachel waved toward the house. "Let's go home, you two."

The two children walked ahead of Rachel, both of them crestfallen.

While her daughter continued to grumble about being forgotten and Andy getting to do everything, Rachel stopped Micah, watching the children move a little farther away. "That driver of Graden's—"

"Two-bits Perez?"

"He and Smitty Jones—I don't know if you remember him—"

"The handyman who worked for you?"

She nodded. "They took the boys." She reached out and grasped Micah's arm. "They got in the truck, and they could have been taken them God knows where instead of for ice cream. Graden threatened me with this very thing. He wasn't a stranger, he said. And he isn't. Look what happened. He wants me to know that he could get to my children or my father anywhere, any time. Next time..." She took a shuddering breath. "There can't be a next time. They can't stay here. It's too dangerous."

"I agree." He clasped her hand. "I'll talk to Kelmen." He looked away, then back at her. "I promise you, I'll take care of it."

That promise was the only thing that convinced Rachel it was okay to go to work.

She had left the children in his, Erin's and Nico's care instead of taking them to her father's to spend the night. They'd been excited about the games Erin had promised them, and Rachel had been thankful the real reason for the change was lost on her children. Micah had told her that he planned to spend part of the evening with her dad, which was another reassurance that her family was being watched over.

When Rachel came out of Shepherd's Inn at nearly one in the morning, Micah was waiting for her, which she expected since he had driven her to work. What she hadn't expected was how happy she was to see him. As she walked across the parking lot toward him, she thought about his promise.

Had he been successful at convincing Kelmen to let her and the children disappear for a while? She had to believe that Micah would find a way to get them into a safe house.

And then what? Once more her father's admonition echoed through her head. And then what? With sudden clarity, she realized the only way she'd ever have her life back was to stay here and somehow finish the business with Graden.

If that didn't happen, she imagined that she'd spend the rest of her life trying to keep one step ahead of the man. For as long as she lived, she never again wanted to be as frightened for her children as she had been today.

"Hi," Micah said, getting out of the vehicle and coming around to the passenger side to open the door. "Was your evening okay?"

"It was. Especially since I have a hundred dollars in tips." She climbed into the vehicle, and was at once struck with how ordinary the conversation sounded— as though they really *did* have a relationship. She stole a glance at him, considering that.

He'd told her that he liked his job, which meant if she had any notion of knowing him after all this was over, she'd have to come to terms with what he did for a living.

"Do you work undercover a lot?" she asked him after they were under way.

"Not as much as I used to." He patted the hair showing beneath his hat. "I'm beginning to look too old for most jobs. A guy like Nico fits into a lot of different operations. He can look like a student from an ivy league school or a homeless guy, like he's Asian or Hispanic."

"You're not that old," she felt compelled to point out though she didn't know exactly how old he was. Forty, maybe, if he was even that.

"I'm not," he agreed, "but your son going missing this afternoon took about ten years off my life."

"So most of the time it's investigative work?"

"It is." He gave her a considering look, but answered without pausing. "Talking to people and poring over paperwork, and searching through thousands of records to find the one detail that makes or breaks a case." He looked from the road to her. "Why are you so curious?"

"I just…" What? She thought. She couldn't very well confess how personal her interest really was. "Was curious," she finished, the excuse sounding beyond lame. "Did you get hold of your boss?"

"Yep."

That statement came out so short that Rachel was positive it hadn't gone well.

"I've been thinking about all this stuff with Graden, and the one thing that I keep coming back to—I mean besides the fact that I don't have his money—is that I'll be looking over my shoulder for the rest of my life if he isn't put out of business."

"You've got that right."

She sighed, appreciating that he agreed with her, but more than a little scared by it, too. "I'm tired of being a victim, Micah. So tell me. Exactly what do we do to get him?"

"Exactly?"

She nodded sharply. "That's right. Right now, he's pulling all the strings, and I'm sick of being his puppet. So, yeah. I want to know what we have to do to get control of this thing. You've done this kind of thing lots of times before. What's next?"

Micah didn't answer, but instead pulled into the nearly deserted parking lot of the City Market where he shut off the engine.

"You've just put your finger on the problem with this operation. Normally, we put a huge amount of time into planning a case, and we try to cover everything we can think of, going in with our bases covered. I came here with one objective—to get you and your children out of harm's way while the rest of us worked the case." He took a breath, his gaze straying to the dark street in front of them. "Taking Graden down is Kelmen's case. Until he threatened you, we didn't have a single solid link between Graden and the operation that sent Angela to prison. So, Kelmen wanted you involved."

"You didn't?"

Micah shook his head, taking off his hat and tossing it behind the seat. "No. I wanted you as far from this mess as possible."

The expression in his eyes transfixed her when he caught her gaze. She couldn't have looked away if her life depended on it. He reached for her hand.

"Having you somewhere safe isn't enough, Rachel." His voice grew husky. "I want you to have your life back and your dreams coming true."

"I don't even remember them anymore," she whispered, her own voice clogging.

He leaned closer, lacing their fingers together. "A house filled with laughter, good friends and good food," he said, as though he had memorized the words. "A bed-and-breakfast where guests can enjoy their morning coffee on a patio surrounded by flowers and mountain views."

She remembered the conversation. They had been shoveling a late-spring snow off the loading dock at the shop, and he'd asked her what she'd be doing if she didn't have the antique business. On that day, she hadn't imagined that within a few short weeks her life would be shattered and her business gone.

He leaned a little closer, his hand warm around her own. "I miss your laughter, Rachel."

She missed it, too, she realized, her free hand coming up to cup his cheek. Last spring she had been falling in love with this man, and she had begun to imagine a life with him. Maybe she'd never have that, but the feelings she had for him had pushed their way through her anger. She didn't want to make the same mistake—holding back instead of admitting what she wanted for the two of them. Without conscious thought, she put her hand behind his neck and pulled him toward her until she could kiss him.

Her eyes drifted shut, and the tears that had made her eyes gritty a moment before softened into something smoother, darker, more gentle. More lovely. He sighed. Or maybe she did. All she knew for certain was that she wanted to hang onto this moment, this feeling where everything was soft and without worry. And his kiss. She had dreamed about this. It was more wonderful than she had imagined.

His hands touched her hair, her cheek, and when the kiss ended, he said, "I've been wanting to kiss you since the first day I met you." His lips brushed over hers in the softest caress that promised everything, asked for nothing. "I was so sure I had lost my chance."

"Me, too," she whispered.

"It was worth the wait."

A balloon of joy expanded through her chest, making her smile. "Maybe, but six months is a long time."

"Who are we talking about here. You? Or me?"

"Me," she whispered, kissing him again. "You're a cruel, cruel man, Micah McLeod, to have kept me from this all these long months."

He tucked her head against his neck, and they sat in the warm silence, watching the sparse traffic that came down the street now and then.

Little by little her thoughts returned to the present and the immense problem of Simon Graden. "I do want to put an end to this," she murmured without raising her head.

"This?"

She could feel the vibration of his voice against her skin.

"Not this." She rested a hand over his heart to reassure him. "Graden."

"We will. Tomorrow morning we'll put a plan in place, get the kids and your dad to safety, and take charge."

How simple he made it all sound. She knew that it wasn't, but how she wanted it to be.

"The fact that you haven't been undercover complicates things, doesn't it?" She sat up so she could look at him.

"It does, but we'll figure out something."

"Maybe," she mused, "I should call Graden and tell him that you're breathing down my back and that I've been forced to choose between a rock and a hard place."

"Which am I now?" Micah asked with a grin.

She swatted at him, feeling happy despite it all. "Be nice. I'm trying to make a plan here. Give the inexperienced one on the team a break, would you?"

"Actually, it's not a bad plan," he assured her. "And, it has the added advantage of being close to the truth."

"So," she concluded. "All I have to do is come up with a half-million dollars in cash."

"That's where I come in," he told her. "I've already filled out a voucher requesting it, and as soon as Kelmen approves it, we should have it."

Once more the whole thing sounded so simple. She imagined that she'd waltz into a bank or some other neutral place, give Graden his money, and have the DEA agents swoop down like superheroes, saving the day.

"And then you'll be leaving," she murmured.

"I've got some time off coming," he told her, taking her hand once more. "Maybe after all this is over you'd like to come see what the Tetons look like in the autumn."

Possibilities shimmered through her as she stared at him, the midnight gloom in the vehicle making it impossible to read his expression. With all the disappointments that had crashed one on top of another these last months, she couldn't risk hoping.

But she did anyway.

ELEVEN

"The safe house for your dad and your kids is set up," Micah told Rachel the following morning.

In a replay of the previous morning, Erin had been sitting at the kitchen table when Rachel got up. This morning, Nico and Micah were with her, as well, and the three of them looked as though they had been talking for a while.

"That's good." The relief that expanded through Rachel at Micah's announcement felt like a lead apron being lifted from her chest.

Her eyes caught Micah's and held, and she vividly remembered the kisses they had shared last night, so much so that she felt transparent. Her gaze slid to Erin, then Nico. Neither of them seemed to notice anything though Erin was smiling.

"You look as though the weight of the world has just been taken off your shoulders," she said.

"It has." Rachel poured herself a cup of coffee from the half-full pot and joined the others at the table. "Do I need to get the kids up?"

"They can sleep for a while yet, but that's up to you," Micah said. "Is your dad an early riser?"

"Even more than I am," Rachel said. "I'll call him. In fact, I should go see him instead." Getting him and the kids to safety was her first concern, but she was also weary of being at odds with him. This was her chance to try to clear the air between them before they left.

Glad as she was to know her dad and her children would all be safe, the next few days suddenly loomed empty. She had never spent a night away from the kids, not counting the occasional sleepover that Sarah had with her friend Amelia.

"When do they leave? Where are they going?" It just then occurred to her that she probably needed to do laundry for them before they left.

"Nico's taking them to my ranch," Micah said.

She had no doubt the kids would love it, and since Micah had told her that his parents lived there, her dad would have company as well. She was also positive that Micah wouldn't have picked his home if he didn't think it was safe.

"Nico? Not you?" Even as she asked the question, the plan felt right to Rachel. She could see the place in her mind's eye, so vivid had been his descriptions of the place.

"That's right," Micah said. "I'm staying here with you. Your idea last night was a good plan, Rachel. It sticks close to the truth, and it's easy for Graden to check out since he'll undoubtedly be expecting a double cross."

"I hadn't thought of that."

He smiled. "Give the senior member of the team some credit, okay?"

The statement was such an echo of what she had said to him last night that she was once more reminded that somehow over the last forty-eight hours she had cast aside her distrust and her long-held anger.

The insight had her turning inward as the other three discussed details around her.

So this is what forgiveness feels like, she thought. Over the last several months, her dad had urged her to forgive Micah, to forgive Angela, and most of all, to forgive herself. She'd been so caught up in her need to be right that she hadn't understood.

Staring unseeingly at her hands, she listened to the ebb and flow of conversation around her, once more testing her feelings. To her great relief, the anger toward Micah was gone. If anyone had told her she'd feel this way, even yesterday morning, she wouldn't have believed it.

"Rachel, is that okay with you?"

Not even sure who had asked the question, she looked up and found the three of them looking at her expectantly.

"I'm sorry. What?" she asked.

"We were just saying that we ought to have them on the road by ten or a little after so they can make most of the drive in daylight."

She glanced outside where it was just beginning to be light. Only four more hours before they'd be on their way. Having them go was the right thing, absolutely. Still, a lump in her throat made swallowing impossible.

Erin reached for her hand. "It'll be okay."

Rachel nodded. "I know. And I want them to go. I

really do." She sniffed. "It's just that I've never been away from them for longer than about twelve hours." Forcing herself to smile, she stood. "And, there are only about sixteen dozen things that need to be done before they go."

"Then maybe you ought to go see your dad first thing. He probably has some things to wrap up to get ready, too," Micah said.

"Give me a list, and we'll take care of those sixteen dozen things you mentioned," said Erin.

Twenty minutes later, Rachel pulled into the driveway at her father's house. The sun was just coming up, glinting off the upstairs windows.

As she shut off the engine, she studied the simple lines of the small house, remembering how big it had seemed to her as a child and how she'd never once doubted her father's love for her or his support of her the way so many of her friends had with their parents. She'd never doubted it, but she had often felt as though she had to stand in line for his time and attention.

In an odd way, that was what had drawn her and Angela together. They'd been sisters of the heart then, bound by the death's of their mothers, Rachel's to cancer and Angela's to an aneurism. Angela's father had been completely inattentive, a man who worked too much and drank too much and left his daughter to fend for herself. Rachel's had been a polar opposite, but she still understood that deep need to have your father really see her and accept you. Her dad accepted her, but to this day, she wasn't sure if he really saw her. Even as a child, she'd understood the importance of his work, and she'd felt selfish when she wished he had more time for her. Not once had Rachel made waves for her dad, though she'd sometimes wondered what would have happened if she had taken a walk on the wild side.

Her dad must have heard her car because the front door opened, and behind the storm door, she could see him watching her. Suddenly nervous, she got out of the car. She didn't want him to leave with their disagreements still hanging between them, but she also worried about telling him what was really in her heart. *Nothing new there.*

He opened the door, a smile on his face. He always smiled when he first saw her, she realized, that earlier lump in her throat back again. Despite all her anger toward him, he always smiled. How could she have not noticed before now?

"You're bright and early," he said as she came up the front steps.

"I had to be." She came through the door. "We've made plans to get you and the children away for a few days."

"I figured that would probably happen today." He kissed her on the cheek as she passed him.

That made her stop and face him. "That must have been some talk you and Micah had."

"You okay with this?" he asked, letting go of the door.

Once more unable to speak because of the clogging emotion in her throat, she nodded. He held out his arms, and she moved into them, needing the comfort just as much as she had when she was a child.

As always, his hugs were sheltering, as though she

had come home again. That thought reminded her of her words to Micah yesterday about being tired of being a victim and of her biggest worry—the imminent fore-closure of the mortgage on her house. Giving up her home would mean moving back here for a while, and though she knew her dad wouldn't mind, every single thing about that felt as if she had failed herself and her children.

She hugged him hard, then stepped away. "Is there any chocolate milk in the fridge?"

He smiled at her request for her childhood favorite. "You know there is. Help yourself."

After pouring the milk, she followed her dad to the backyard to the stone bench overlooking his flower garden, which was bursting with its late-summer blooms. She didn't sit, somehow missing the swing set that had been where the bench now sat.

"You look like you're bursting at the seams to tell me something," her dad said. "Sarah gets that very same expression on her face."

The time and attention he gave to her children was one more thing to add to her list of things to be thankful for, she thought. "I'm glad you agreed to go with the kids."

"I sure don't like leaving you behind. When Micah and I talked about this yesterday after Andy came home, he said you needed to stay here."

"It's a scary thing, Dad, but it's the only way I'm going to get my life back." She met his gaze. "He wants you guys to leave this morning, so as soon as I go back home, I've got to get the kids ready."

"You don't have much time."

"Micah, Nico and Erin are helping out. So you're already packed?"

"A man my age doesn't need much. My Bible and a few changes of clothes is all." He tapped a finger against one of the tubes of a wind chime hanging from the tall shepherd's hook next to the bench, releasing a couple of sweet-sounding notes. "You could have called me—"

"I needed to talk to you."

"I've been praying that you would."

She had no doubt about that. "I really hate that we've been at odds with each other these last few weeks."

"I know that." His eyes were bright when he looked at her. "I've disliked it, too."

She took a sip of her milk, no longer sure at all what she wanted to say to him and yearning for some *thing* she couldn't even name.

"You don't seem as tense despite everything going on."

"I think that's because of the decision I made yesterday." She sat next to him, setting the glass down. "I'm tired of being a victim, Dad."

"That's good. A good first step. Being a victim is a choice that only you can change."

Something in his tone made her think he'd slipped away from being her dad and into being a minister, which was so much a part of him. Inseparable as he had often told her they were, right now she wanted only her dad.

Ignoring that niggling discontent, she added, "I've decided to put my house up for sale."

"Another good step," he murmured. "A new beginning. A way to start clean again."

"Stop it." She rose to her feet, the frustration suddenly spilling out. "I want you to tell me that you know it hurts me and that you know I'm scared. It's *not* a good first step. There's nothing good about it except for getting rid of the mortgage. It's giving up dreams and admitting that I'm not making enough money and so I'm going to have to ask you if we can move back here only I'd rather cut off an arm than do that because it means that I'm not able to take care of my children by myself and—"

To her horror, she burst into tears, the outburst making her feel as though she were ten and still seeking her father's approval instead of an adult doing adult things and making responsible adult decisions.

He stood and gathered her close, which only made her cry harder.

"Everything about you and your children and your life is important to me, Rachel."

"I know. I do know that." She stepped out of his embrace swiping at her eyes. "But, do you have any idea how lonely it is when I come here looking for my dad and instead find my minister?"

"I can't separate one from the other," he replied. "You've always known that. I only want what's best for you."

"You want what's best for everyone," she countered, "so that hardly sets me apart from anyone else. Do you remember that book you gave me a few months ago— the one about regaining faith?"

"Of course, I remember," he said. "I thought it would help you find a path back to yours."

"It made me feel like I needed to be fixed, like what

I was feeling wasn't okay, like I had no reason to be so angry with Angela—"

"I was just trying to help."

"I didn't *want* help. I wanted my dad just to be there for once and just to listen without expecting me to be the model daughter. Instead, you gave that understanding to Angela."

"My extending a helping hand to another doesn't hurt you," he said.

"How do you know what hurts and what doesn't hurt, Dad? Trust me, it hurts every single time you go to see her, and I'm left wishing that just once you'd see me as needing your compassion and your understanding just as much as she does."

"You don't think you have those?" He sounded incredulous.

"No. I don't."

He extended a hand toward her. "So, we're back to square one again."

"Yes." She picked up the glass of milk and turned toward the kitchen. "I've got to go. I'll give you a call when Nico heads this way to pick you up."

He nodded, following her into the house.

She set the glass in the sink, then turned around once more, meeting his gaze, his eyes as sad as she felt. "I'm sorry for yelling, Dad."

"I love you, Rachel."

She knew that he did. She wished it were enough to heal the breach between them.

"I love you, too, Dad," she whispered right before she fled.

* * *

"Here's your mail," Micah said to Rachel about an hour after Nico had driven away with Sarah, Andy and her father.

She already missed them, and the only way to deal with that was to stay too busy to mope. Her cleaning project, however, didn't keep her from replaying the conversation with her father in her head.

"Just set it on the table." She had retreated to the kitchen where she had decided to scrub the floor. At the moment, she was diligently attacking the last of the grime at the threshold by the back door.

A moment later, Micah dropped to his haunches next to her and pulled the toothbrush from her hand. "I think you have that spot clean."

"You think I'm being a little compulsive?"

He ducked his head, coming into her line of vision, a smile in his eyes. "Are you going to hit me if I tell you the truth?"

"Probably." She felt the corner of her mouth lift. "Sending them away…"

"Is the right thing, Rachel, just as it was a week ago when you wanted to do the same thing." He pulled her to her feet. "You've called Graden and left a message for him. There's a tap on your phone, and all we can do now is wait."

"I'm terrible at waiting." She glanced back at the spotless floor. "And all of this cleaning really does have a purpose. I've decided to put the house up for sale."

"You're sure about that? I know how much you love this place."

She stared at him, hearing the compassion in his voice, the understanding that she'd been hoping for from her father. Swallowing, she said, "I do love it. But I can't afford to keep it. Realistically, I'll have to spend a huge amount of money to get it up to code to turn it into a bed-and-breakfast like I want, and that's assuming I can get the city council to approve the zoning change required to do it." She looked around the room, her gaze landing on the mail. The letter on the top had a return address from the mortgage company, and since she was now sixty days behind on her payments, she was positive it was a foreclosure warning. "It's time to stop hanging onto the past and dreams that will never be."

"So what's the new dream, Rachel?"

"I don't know." She smiled at him, remembering how he had asked almost the same thing the other day. "I'm still working on that."

Micah longed to pull her into his arms and urge her to consider a dream that might include him. After finally having her in his arms last night, he wanted her there again more than ever. He'd be lying to himself, though, if he allowed himself to think their current situation was anything more than a temporary truce. His betrayal last spring couldn't be so easily forgiven.

"Hey, Micah, come take a look at this," Erin called from the study.

Aware that Rachel was following him, he found Erin keeping an eye on the camera monitors they had installed yesterday after the graffiti incident. A flashy sports car had parked on the street a couple of houses away, the shadowy image of a driver visible from inside. A second later he got out of the vehicle.

"That's Tommy Manderoll," Rachel said, confirming what Micah already knew.

And he was heading for the house.

"Do you want him to know you're here?" Rachel asked Micah.

"Erin's got a good cover story for being here. I don't." He headed for the back door. "I'll check in with the two of you later."

"Okay." Rachel watched him go down the side of the garage and through the gate. "I wonder what Tommy wants."

Had Graden sent him, she wondered. She hadn't been all that surprised Graden hadn't picked up this morning when she'd called. Since she had threatened him yesterday morning, it made sense he didn't want to talk to her.

A second later the front door bell rang. She glanced back at Erin, who smiled reassuringly. Rachel headed for the door and pulled it open.

"Hey, Rachel." Tommy smiled, then made a point of looking back at the street as though he expected to see someone.

"Hey, yourself," she said without pushing open the screen door to let him in. "What do you want?"

"Is that any way to talk to a friend? Make him stand here on the porch without even an offer of a cold drink?"

"I don't see any friends on my porch," Rachel said.

He leaned closer. "Maybe. But our mutual *friend* is

very unhappy with you." He shrugged. "Maybe you want to talk on the porch. Maybe you don't."

She held open the door and he came in, his attention on the hallway beyond her. "Well, well, well. Who is this?"

Rachel turned around to look at Erin, who had done something to her hair in the last thirty seconds to make it stand up in the same spiky style she'd had the day she'd seen her in the pool hall. She'd also tied the tails of the oxford shirt she'd been wearing over her T-shirt into a halter that emphasized her slim form and made her look like she had nothing more on her mind than a good time.

"I'm Erin," she said in a breathy voice. She sauntered forward and extended her hand. "Didn't Rachel tell you? She's renting me a room. And who are you?"

"Tommy Manderoll, at your service." He took her hand and instead of shaking it, twirled her around. "Haven't I seen you around?"

"Maybe. I've been hanging here and there. You know how it is when you're trying to meet new people. You've got to be seen."

"And, honey, do I see you."

"Oh, please. Tommy, give it a rest," Rachel said to him. "Have you forgotten about your last girlfriend? The one who went to prison because of you?"

Erin batted her eyes. "No. You don't look like a man who could do such a thing."

"She's in prison, but not because of me." When Erin subtly pulled her hand out of his, he looked at Rachel.

"You had something you wanted to talk to me

about." She motioned toward the kitchen. "Maybe over that cold drink you said you wanted."

He looked back at Erin. "Want to go out on the town when I'm done talking to Rachel?"

Erin gave him a flirty smile. "Sure. I don't have anything else to do. I'd like to have somebody show me where the hot spots are."

"And I can't wait to show you," he said.

In the kitchen, Rachel plunked ice cubes into a glass, amazed at Erin's transformation. One minute she was the girl next door, and the next a vamp. Though Rachel supposed it was part of the job, the shift reminded her that as much as she liked Erin, she didn't know her or understand how she could do her job any more than she understood how Micah did his.

"I like your friend," Tommy said. "When did she get in town?"

"A couple of days ago." Stick to the truth, she reminded herself, following Micah's advice. Don't volunteer anything, and answer only what's asked. Rachel handed him a glass of tea. "Get to the point and tell me what you want."

"I'm supposed to get some sort of proof that you have Graden's money."

So Graden had gotten her message, she thought.

She shook her head. "You don't think I'm just going to have a half-million dollars lying around my house, do you?"

"What I think is that you're in way over your head and that Graden will eat you up and spit you out if you mess with him." He strolled toward the window that overlooked the backyard. "He knows that McLeod has been here."

"That's been no secret."

"Are you a suspect?"

"That makes it sound like I've committed a crime."

"Are you?" Tommy repeated.

"That's what he implied when he was here the other day," she said.

Tommy turned back from the window and looked at her. "I figure there's only one way you could have gotten hold of a half-million dollars. You double-crossed me the other day and picked up the package at the hotel after all. Which means you don't know a thing about street value or keeping your word or—"

"I told you the truth. I didn't go to work because I got fired. So I wasn't there to pick up your package and I don't know anything about that or what might have happened to it."

"I'm not sure I believe you."

"I can't help that," Rachel said.

"Hey, Tommy, are you going to keep a girl waiting all day?" Erin appeared in the doorway. She had put on makeup and carried a small purse under her arm.

"I'll be right there," he said. "Just give me a minute."

She winked. "I'll be waiting for you on the porch."

He sauntered toward Rachel. "Because of Angela, I'm going to do you a favor and tell Graden I've seen proof you have the money."

"Why would you do that?"

"Because I know you, preacher's daughter. You can't lie without giving yourself away." He headed toward the hallway, then turned around. "And if you could, I'd be as good as dead, and I know you wouldn't want that on your conscience."

TWELVE

After Tommy and Erin left, Rachel went back to the kitchen where her floor-scrubbing project held even less allure than it had before. She dumped the cleaning water and put her supplies away.

The house was too quiet, too empty. She hated her morose thoughts that were circling from her family and their journey to Graden and his demands to Tommy and his strange visit to Erin's transformation and back to her family.

And she wondered what she was supposed to do next.

For months her every waking hour had been so full that to find herself with *any* free time was disconcerting. Weird. What had she done when she had free time? She didn't even remember.

The telephone rang, startling her.

Dreading that it might be Graden on the end of the line, hoping it would be so all this would soon be over, she let the phone ring twice more while she composed her thoughts.

"Is everything okay, Rachel?" Micah asked after she answered. "You sound funny."

"I was expecting you to be Gra—"

"That's a call I don't want you to get while you're by yourself. I've picked up a few groceries at the City Market. Would you like to come get me?"

"Sure."

"And just so you know, I'm going to sit on the floor in the back seat of your car. I'd rather only you and Erin know I'm at your house."

"Okay."

She had a new appreciation for his caution when she spotted an unfamiliar car at the end of the block. A guy was sitting behind the wheel, ostensibly reading a newspaper. He caught her eye when she came by.

Shivers slid down her back, and the whole way to the store, she kept looking in her rearview mirror expecting to see the vehicle.

At the store, she found Micah standing in the shade, and he got into the car the instant she came to a stop.

"Did you hear from Erin yet?" Rachel asked when they were underway again. Behind her, Micah had settled with his back against the passenger-side back door, his legs stretched in front of him.

"She called right after Tommy arrived at your place telling me that she'd talked him into taking her out. If anyone can find out what he's really up to, it's Erin."

"I think he's somebody who wants to be a big shot but isn't."

"That's my take on him, too," Micah said, "which doesn't necessarily keep him from being dangerous."

"There was a guy who seemed to be watching the house," Rachel said, relating what little there was to tell. "The scary part is that I probably would have never noticed him a day or two ago."

"I bet you would have," he reassured her. "With your kids out playing…you strike me as the kind of woman who knows exactly what's going down in her neighborhood."

Turning into the alley behind her house, she hit the remote control to open the garage door. It went up, and as she drove into the garage, she saw there was a sheet of hot-pink paper hanging from the drive mechanism at the top center of the door.

Someone had gotten into the garage to put it there. She stopped the vehicle, staring into the gloom even though there was no place for someone to hide inside the building.

Micah had also seen the sheet because he asked, "Was this here when you left?"

She shook her head. "I don't think so. That would have been a little hard to miss."

The garage appeared to be empty except for the lawn mower sitting off to one side. The paint and yard supplies on the shelves at the back of the garage looked just as they always had.

"What do you want me to do?" she asked, torn by indecision.

"Drive in, then close the door," he said. "It will make retrieving the paper easier."

She did, and he got out of the car. When he brought the sheet back to her, she immediately noticed that he had put on a latex glove and was holding it by the corner.

"Graden has taken the bait," he said as Rachel got out of the car. "He wants you to meet him." He held out the note for her to read. The message was typewritten and terse. Iron Mountain Tram, Sunday, 9:00 a.m.

"On Sunday morning?" she asked. "I didn't know that it ran then."

"That's because you're a woman who goes to church."

He was right. She was, even though she hadn't set foot inside the sanctuary for months until the other day. While others worshiped inside, she sat in the garden, listening to the music and wondering how to get her life out of survival mode.

Micah handed Rachel one of the sacks of groceries, then went to the side door, opening it, and doing a visual search of the yard before saying, "Give me your keys so I can unlock the house. Did you set the alarm before you left?"

She nodded.

"I'm still going to search the house—need to make sure our visitor wasn't inside." He glanced back at her. "You stay put in the kitchen, so I know where you are, okay?"

Once more she nodded, this time with dread dropping to the bottom of her toes.

They hurried to the back door, and when they were inside, he disappeared to the front of the house while she turned off the alarm.

He was quiet, but she knew when he'd stepped into

her bedroom upstairs because she heard the tell-tale creak of the floor in front of the closet door. A few seconds later he came back into the kitchen, a smile on his face.

"All clear." He squeezed her shoulder as he came past her and flipped the lock for the back door. "You're a rare woman." At her raised eyebrow, he grinned and added, "One who stays put when asked."

She managed a smile as she began pulling groceries from the sack. "I've seen that movie, and I know how that turns out."

"What can you tell me about the Iron Mountain Tram?" he asked.

"It goes straight up the mountain to the Fairy Caves and an adventure park." She frowned. "Does he mean meet him at the bottom of the tram or in a car?"

Unloading another sack of groceries, Micah said, "The note didn't say. I figured I'd need to get up there to scout things out."

"There's no way I'm getting into one of those cars, much less with him. Some people might think dangling a thousand feet in the air is fun, but I don't."

"I bet the views are great."

"There are great views all over the place, and you can catch most of them with both feet firmly planted on the ground."

"You don't have a problem with heights, do you? We did take that hike that was pretty straight up the other day."

"A major difference there is I walking and had a hand rail to hang onto." She shook her head. "A tram is hanging from a cable—and yes, I know those things get inspected and cars are supposed to be locked so you can't fall out and all that, but still, thanks, but no thanks."

"Tell me what you remember about the parking lot for the tram."

Rachel did, feeling more nervous by the minute. "Is this going to be one of those deals where I have to personally hand over the money? Can you imagine trying to do business this way? Any sort of business. What ever happened to good old electronic transfers?"

"That works if you don't mind the transaction being traced. And I'm betting Graden wants the cash for some reason." He clapped his hands together. "I hope you're hungry for pizza."

"What about going to check out the tram?"

"Later. Right now, I'm hungry. It's been forever since breakfast. Plus, I figure you need something to occupy your mind."

"Strange ingredients for pizza," she told him, allowing the subject to change as she took in the things he had left on the counter. "French bread, spaghetti sauce, fresh mushrooms."

He handed her the package of mushrooms. "Your job is to saute these in a little butter and olive oil."

"I didn't know you cooked," she said.

He suddenly came close, lightly tipped her chin up with his knuckle, and kissed her. "There are a lot of things you don't know about me, Rachel Neesham. And I aim to change that."

"You do?" Her breath escaped from her body, leaving behind a giddiness that made her want to laugh.

He grinned, then kissed her again. "Oh, yeah. I do."

Something about that *I do* reached into her heart and made her imagine him saying it as a vow. A very dangerous idea, but one that lingered anyway.

"When do you think we'll hear from Erin?" she asked, deliberately steering her thoughts to a safer subject.

"When we hear," he said. "And you're trying to change the subject. You're supposed to ask me what I'm going to be doing while you saute the mushrooms."

There was no way to resist his lighthearted mood. "Okay, I bite. What—"

"I'm glad you asked." He came to stand behind her and put his arms around her waist. "I'm going to supervise. And since the mushrooms are tender, I figure I'd better be close to make sure you don't burn them." He kissed her cheek.

I'm in love with him. The realization vibrated through her heart like the chimes in her dad's backyard, deep, resonating tones that she could feel to her toes. She closed her eyes and leaned into him, his cheek warm against hers as his hands left her waist and slid down her arms.

"You're not paying attention," he whispered teasingly.

She opened her eyes and found that he was stirring the mushrooms. Reclaiming her concentration she took the wooden spoon from him. He squeezed her shoulder then stepped away.

"Want a soda or anything?" he asked.

"Iced tea," she murmured, doing her best to concentrate on the task in front of her, but her thoughts racing ahead as she imagined a future with him. Too easily she saw it all.

Micah, teasing her and being with her while they cooked, as they were now.

Micah, playing with her children they way they all liked so much.

Micah, understanding her the way no one else seemed to.

Micah…walking out of her life when this job was done.

The sense of loss that thought brought was all too real, though it hadn't happened.

Yet.

The teeter-totter of her emotions made her want to curl into a ball so she could protect her vulnerable core, or grab onto him, begging him to never, ever leave. Neither was acceptable, so she merely stood there stirring the fragrant mushrooms as though everything in her world was totally okay.

"Those smell great." He set the iced tea on the counter next to the stove. "A little sausage, a little garlic, and we'll be set." He brushed another of those sweet, casual kisses on her cheek.

"Ah." And she savored this feeling, tucking it away to remember later.

They had just finished eating, a meal they had taken to the secluded backyard patio where the balmy air had the barest hint of a chill, when Micah's cell phone rang.

"McLeod," he answered.

Rachel watched him as his expression changed to all business, his eyes suddenly intent, dark, as he listened to whatever he was being told by the caller.

A frisson of worry slid through her. Surely this wasn't about her family. Surely they were all okay. She glanced at her watch, noting they were probably a couple of hours from their destination yet.

"Okay," he said, and clipped closed the phone. When his gaze met hers, his eyes were troubled. "That was Erin. She's at the emergency room."

Rachel rose to her feet. "What happened? Is she okay?"

He didn't answer right away, and her concern ratcheted up several notches.

"Micah? Did Tommy do something to her?"

"I don't know." He raked a hand through his hair. "I've got to go, and I don't want to take you with me, but I don't want you here alone, either."

"How badly is she hurt?"

His eyes darkened. "I don't know."

She gathered up their dishes. "Let's get this stuff inside and let's go."

He opened the door, then followed her into the house.

"She's supposedly my tenant." She set the dishes on the counter. "I have a reason to go. Maybe you should stay and I'll go."

His frown deepened. "That's not how it works, Rachel. She's an agent on my team, and—"

"And that makes you responsible."

"Yes."

"Give me a sec to get a sweater, and I'm ready."

Micah watched her go, knowing her reaction to the situation was the only one possible. She was back in nothing flat, locking the door, and leaving him without a plan to leave her here.

"Did she tell you what happened?" Rachel asked the minute they were in the car with Micah driving.

"She was a little vague about that," he hedged. According to Erin, Tommy had been badly beaten. Things like that didn't happen in Rachel's world, and the truth was, he didn't want her even to know about this kind of violence.

As if realizing he didn't want to talk, Rachel took his hand, her head bowed as though she might be praying. He hoped she was, even though she'd been pretty specific that she and God weren't talking right now. Squeezing her hand, he refocused his own thoughts into prayer for Erin, for Tommy and for this whole situation to end without any more harm coming to anyone.

Inside the hospital emergency room, they were directed to a curtained cubicle where Erin was propped up on a hospital bed. She had a nasty-looking scrape on her cheekbone, and her arm was in a sling.

"Oh, Erin," Rachel said while Micah gruffly asked, "Are you okay?"

Erin gave them both a cheerful grin. "You should see the other guy."

"Don't give me that," Rachel said. "You look like you've been in a fist fight."

"Not intentionally. Just got a little too close to one." To

Micah, Erin added, "You might want to check on Tommy."

"He was involved in this?" Rachel asked, planting her hands on her hips. "I might have known. He didn't hit you, did he?"

"No. Nothing like that."

"I'll be back in a minute," Micah said, stepping outside the cubicle. On the far side of the room, a cop stood in front of a curtain.

Micah crossed the room, removing his ID from his pocket. "Is Tommy Manderoll in there?" he asked, handing his wallet to the officer.

He glanced briefly at the identification, then said, "Yes, sir, he is."

"What can you tell me?"

"Not much to tell. I'm just here to take the man's statement."

"He's not being charged?" Micah asked.

"No. The way the little lady over there told it," he said waving in the direction of the cubicle where Erin was, "is that he was just defending himself against a couple of other guys. Just another Saturday-night bar fight according to the witnesses."

"Thanks." Micah slipped through the curtain.

He hardly recognized the man. His face was a mass of cuts and contusions that would become swollen bruises within another few hours. One eye was swollen shut, and a butterfly bandage was holding his left eyebrows together.

Tommy opened an eye. When he saw Micah, he said, "Great. More trouble."

"Did Graden do this to you?" Micah asked.

"Talking to you could be a life-shortening proposition. Go away."

"You must not be hurt too bad since you're still a smart aleck."

Tommy motioned for Micah to come closer. "They made your girl." At Micah's scowl, he added, "Don't give me that confused look, Special Agent McLeod. You know very well who I mean. And whatever game you've gotten Rachel involved with—it's a thousand times more dangerous than anything I ever did with Angela." His voiced faded as he talked, as though it had required every ounce of his energy.

"What do you mean? C'mon, man, talk straight to me."

"I am being straight," Tommy said fiercely. "And when I get out of here, I figure a trip is in order. Disappear for a while and give Simon Graden time to forget about me."

That confirmed to Micah what he suspected—this wasn't just another bar fight. He wouldn't learn any more until he could talk to Erin. And that was a conversation that needed to be quite a bit more private than a curtained cubicle in the ER.

Micah turned to leave.

"McLeod."

He turned back and met Tommy's bloodshot eye.

"Just so you know. It was never my idea to turn Rachel into a mule. Don't let anything happen to her. She's not tough enough for this game."

At last. Something they agreed about.

The officer poked his head through the curtain. "You ready to sign the complaint, sir?"

"I've changed my mind," Tommy said. "I don't want to press charges."

"The DA will probably take this up with or without your complaint."

"I doubt if I could identify the guys."

"If you're worried about being bullied, the judge will issue a restraining order."

"Like those ever really work," Tommy said.

"If you change your mind…"

"I won't."

The officer shrugged, then left, and Micah headed back to the curtained cubicle where Erin was. The doctor was with her and had decided that she needed a stitch to close the wound on her cheek—the best way to keep it from scarring.

"Where's Rachel?" he asked.

"She said she had to use the restroom," Erin said. "And, she was going to bring me back a cup of water. You didn't see her?"

"No."

He didn't see her anywhere in the larger room where only one other area was curtained off besides where Erin and Tommy were. He peeked into the curtained off area and found only a young mother rocking a sick toddler.

Crossing to the nurses' station, Micah asked, "The woman who came in with me—have you seen her?"

"I didn't see you come in," the nurse said. "Maybe she's in the waiting room."

He strode through the double doors that led back to the waiting room, and Rachel wasn't there, either. Nor was she anywhere else he looked inside or out.

It was as though she had disappeared into thin air.

THIRTEEN

"My goodness," said Reverend Staum, who was walking down the hallway toward the hospital chapel. "To see you twice within a week. That's a pleasure."

"You, too." In search of the restroom, Rachel, still lost in her thoughts, had just left Erin in the care of a nurse who was prepping her for a couple of stitches.

Erin hadn't wanted to talk about the fight Tommy had been in or how she came by her injuries. She had insisted there wasn't anything for Rachel to worry about—it had been a bar fight. That's all. Since Tommy was the kind of guy who often attracted that kind of trouble, Erin's explanation made sense. And that gave Rachel an odd sort of relief. No Simon Graden lurking in the shadows. At least not tonight.

"Is everything okay?" Reverend Staum was asking. "You're not here for your dad or one of the kids?"

"I'm not, thank goodness." Rachel refocused her attention to the minister. "A friend of mine who is staying with me for a few days was in a scuffle." Now that she knew Micah's secret—stick to the truth and don't volunteer anything—she felt a lot more comfortable with how she could respond to others about her activities over the next few days. Still, she longed for it to all be over. "She's going to be fine," Rachel said. "Just a couple of stitches, and she'll be ready to go."

"That's good," he said. "I've just come from visiting Ivy Swanson—you remember her, don't you?"

Rachel did. Mrs. Swanson had been a regular around the church for Rachel's entire life, and she had looked as though she was a hundred for most of that time. She had been living on her own until she'd broken her hip a few weeks ago.

"Since she was admitted to the hospital, she's gone downhill every day. She was transferred to the hospice wing today," he added with a sigh.

"I'll include her in my prayers," Rachel said, surprisingly herself. She hadn't intended to say those words, had she? Even though she'd said them a thousand times before over her life, she hadn't included anyone in her prayers in a long time. The words were intended to provide comfort, but did she intend to pray? She wished she knew.

He smiled as though she had given him a precious gift. "Thank you. You've been in my prayers, too."

She had no idea what to say to that and took a couple of steps toward the waiting room for the ER. Then she remembered his interest in purchasing her home and her own assertion that she wanted to take charge of her life. No time like the present to start practicing what she had been preaching to herself.

"Reverend Staum."

"Yes?" He stopped in mid stride, then stepped out of the way when an orderly came by pushing a patient in a wheelchair.

Rachel glanced back toward the ER weighing her need to talk with him against getting back to Erin and Micah.

"I don't have long, but may I walk with you? I'd like to discuss my house."

"Another prayer answered," he said as they strolled toward the door marked Chapel, a slow smile spreading across his face. He pushed open the door to the dimly lit room. "Assuming you've had a change of heart."

"Are you serious about wanting to buy my house?" she asked when they sat down on one of the pews.

He nodded. "I wouldn't have asked you, but your dad indicated you might be thinking about it."

She sighed, and instead of the familiar tightening in her chest, she felt as though another weight was being lifted from her shoulders. Living with her dad for a while wouldn't be the end of the world, even though they weren't getting along at the moment. They'd have the shared interest of the children. Rachel admitted to herself that Andy and Sarah also provided a great buffer between her and her father.

"It's time to let it go," she said. She laid her hand over his. "Time to have that big house filled with a boisterous family."

Reverend Staum laughed. "That about describes my boys."

They talked a few minutes longer, soon agreeing on

a price and concluding with a promise to meet within the next few days to finalize the details. Reverend Staum was clearly thrilled, which made Rachel happy, as well.

Saying goodbye, she left the reverend and stopped in the hall for a long moment, seeing the world with refreshed eyes. The worry of her home was gone. To have this lifted along with her anger toward Micah filled her with hope that one day soon she'd feel like her old, cheerful self. If only she could as easily eliminate this all-consuming fear of Simon Graden's demands.

One step at a time, she reminded herself.

With that thought, she headed back toward the emergency room. To her complete surprise, Erin wasn't there, nor was Micah. According to the nurse, Erin had been released about ten minutes earlier, and the two of them had left.

Completely dumbfounded that that they had gone without her, Rachel went back to the ER waiting room expecting they might be there. They weren't.

Nor were they outside. Worse, her car was gone.

She dug into her purse for the cell phone that Micah had given her the other day, and flipped it open to call him. The call failed and a message appeared on the display that it had a low battery.

Of course it did, she thought with disgust, since she hadn't remembered to charge it. That was the problem with new devices—remembering the little things that made them work.

Thinking about all the times that her dad had drilled into her head the need to have change for a pay phone, she dug back into her purse. Some pennies. A dime. Not enough to make a call.

Where had Micah and Erin gone? And why in the world had they left without her? The only reasons that she could think of meant Erin had taken a sudden turn for the worse and she really wasn't okay. Except that didn't make any sense. They were in a hospital, so if she'd gotten worse, she would have been admitted. That was her own panic talking, Rachel thought. Not anything sensible.

A worse thought lodged in her head. Something had happened to her family, and that's why they had left. Only that made no sense. Still, she closed her eyes against the pain of that, and for the briefest instant a whisper of the silence chased through her, reminding her of a time when she had trusted in God's eternal good. She stilled, waiting for it to come back. Only it didn't. But somehow, she knew her children were okay.

Once more, she couldn't think of a single reason why Micah and Erin would have gone anywhere without her. Her thoughts raced as she headed back inside to find a telephone.

The receptionist at the information desk gave her a sympathetic look while she explained her predicament.

"You wouldn't believe how often that happens," the woman said, pointing Rachel toward a courtesy phone behind her.

And then she realized she didn't know Micah's number. Getting out the cell phone once more, she opened it. And it was now dead. Low battery, my foot, she thought. Make that a dead battery. But, if Reverend Staum was still here…

She raced outside to the part of the parking lot where there were a couple of reserved parking places for ministers. No vehicles there, either.

Tears of frustration burned at her eyes. No phone, no money, miles from her house.

"Think," she whispered to herself. "Just calm down and think." The adult advice she might give to her daughter in this situation escaped her. The need to do something was overwhelming even as she decided staying here at the hospital was her best option. Sooner or later, Micah would be back. She hoped.

Perhaps they had parked her car someplace else. Deciding it was worth another look, so she went outside once more. And her car still was not in the parking lot. She went out to the street and checked both directions, not seeing anything that gave her a single clue about where Micah might have gone or why he had taken her car. Unreasonable fear accompanied by her worst imaginings alternated with unreasonable anger with him for leaving her.

She'd give them an hour, she finally decided. Make that a half hour. She headed back toward the hospital entrance and the ER waiting room visible through the big windows.

She was nearly to the door when Tommy walked out of the building with slow deliberation, moving as though every single bone hurt. He immediately noticed her. His arm was in a sling, and a bandage covered part of his forehead. His usually immaculate suit looked as bad as he did. At the extent of his obvious pain, her caution gave way to concern.

"Are you sure you should be out here?"

He looked as though he should have been admitted rather than being discharged. One eye was swollen shut, and the rest of his face was battered.

"Who's sure about anything?" he countered, his usual cocky tone in place despite the fatigue in his posture.

"I'm sorry you—"

He held up a hand, and so she stopped in mid sentence.

"I don't want to hear a single thing," he said. "You did what you gotta do, and now so do I."

"What does that mean?"

"I'm leaving town for a while. Too dangerous." He wove a little, and she reached out to steady him. He pointed a finger at her. "Graden has turned into a crazy man, ranting and raving about how he's been done wrong and nobody gets away with cheating him. You should leave, too."

"You almost sound like you care," she said.

He turned, looking at her with his one good eye. "How long have we known each other? Since junior high school?"

"Something like that," she said, wondering what that had to do with anything. The truth was, she had never paid any attention to him until after he and Angela had started dating.

He looked away and sighed. "It wasn't supposed to turn out like this," he said. "I was going to be somebody special."

Once she would have told him that in God's eyes

everyone was special. The preacher's kid, ready to do the good work expected of her. He would have laughed at her when they were kids, and she suspected he still would.

"What? No pious platitudes from you?" The question should have been a sneer, but simply sounded tired.

"We all make our choices," Rachel said.

Just then a cab pulled to a stop in front of them.

"Good. My ride is here." He took a couple of steps toward the curb, then looked back. "Do you need a lift?"

"I—"

"Wait." He made an exaggerated point of looking around. "You came with McLeod didn't you?"

"I—"

"Don't even bother denying it," he interrupted. Then he laughed, a raspy, hollow sound. "Did the DEA agents leave you behind?" His finger came up one more time, this time to chastise her. "Letting that pretty agent go off with me and letting me think she was just a chick out looking for a good time. That wasn't very nice."

So he knew Erin was a special agent. Once more, Rachel had no idea how to respond.

Tommy opened the passenger door of the cab. "Climb in, Rachel. I'll see that you get home. Scout's honor."

She folded her arms over her chest. "How do I know I can trust you?"

"You got a better offer?" He pulled a wad of bills from his pocket and peeled off a couple.

She didn't have a better option, but she didn't like this one, either.

"Take the cab, Rachel. Give the man your address, and get into the car. I don't have all day."

And since she had no better idea, she did just that, positive she couldn't trust Tommy, equally positive this was her best way home.

Tommy leaned in and handed the driver the bills. "The lady's fare. Send me another cab, okay?"

"You've got it, buddy."

Tommy closed the door, then waved at her from the curb when it pulled away.

Stunned at his consideration, Rachel turned around to look at him as the cab turned the corner. And then, bits of their conversation began to make sense. It hadn't been a simple bar fight, after all. Somehow, Graden was behind his beating.

What she'd just seen with Tommy was fear. She'd lived with it long enough to recognize it. Seeing him afraid added another layer to her own worries and rabid imagination.

The taxi took her straight home, just as Tommy had promised.

She took in everything when they reached her block. No unfamiliar cars. Nothing out of place. Her house looked normal with the light in the living room turned on by a timer, just as always. Still, she looked nervously around the block one last time before grabbing the door handle.

Thanking the driver, she got out of the car, retrieved her extra key from the hiding place under one of the bird houses on an old stump in the middle of the yard, and went inside.

After shutting off the alarm system, she plugged the cell phone into its charger and waited impatiently for the next fifteen minutes for it to have enough of a charge that she could turn it on and retrieve Micah's number.

When she dialed it, he answered on the first ring.

"Where are you?" she asked.

"More to the point, where are you?" he countered, his voice harsh.

"At home."

"We'll be there in twenty minutes," he said, disconnecting the call.

"Well, I'm glad that went well," she said staring at the receiver, then setting it down. She realized she was shaking. Where had they gone? Why had they left without her?

The dishes stacked in the sink reminded her of the headlong dash they'd taken out of the house when Erin had called. Unsettled by the anger in Micah's voice, she loaded the dishwasher and straightened the kitchen.

Seventeen minutes later, Rachel heard the garage door open, then close, and from the window above the kitchen sink watched Erin and Micah stride through the dark toward the house.

"Where did you go?" he demanded while Rachel asked, "Is everything okay? Why did you leave without me?"

"What do you mean, where did I go?" she added. "I was at the hospital."

He took off his hat and tossed it toward the table, his expression as black as a thunderhead. "I looked for you. You weren't anywhere."

"I'm going to go take a Tylenol," Erin said, stepping round them.

"Anywhere evidently didn't include the chapel," Rachel said folding her arms over her chest.

Micah raked a hand through his hair and said at the same time, "Do you have any idea how worried I was? You only scared about another ten years off my life."

"Well, double for me," she retorted, closer to tears by far more than she wanted to be. "Why did you leave without me? Where did you go?"

"I didn't think you were there, and we were out looking for you," he ground out. "When you didn't answer the page, I even called the team in Aspen and told them to check Graden's place."

"I never heard the page. I ran into Reverend Staum," she said. "We were in the chapel."

He grabbed her by the shoulders. "The point is you weren't where you were supposed to be and you didn't let anyone know and I couldn't get hold of you on the cell—"

"That's because I forgot to charge the battery." She pointed in the direction of the phone on the shelf.

"Great. Just great. Things fall completely apart because you forgot to charge your phone, and I drive halfway to Aspen because I'm convinced that Graden grabbed you."

He was shouting now, and she was furious with him for scaring her.

"Don't you blame me." She poked a finger in the middle of his chest.

"Why didn't you just call me?" he demanded. "I would have come back to the hospital."

"I don't remember your phone number, Micah." The hurt was back, itching at her like a scab with tender flesh underneath. "And you left. And I had a whole seventeen cents."

"So just how did you get home?"

"Tommy paid for a cab."

"Scum-of-the-earth Tommy? You got in a car with him after what happened to Erin? That was definitely a stupid idea."

"I didn't get in a car with him, and if I'd had a better idea, I would have done it." She held out her hand. "I want my keys back."

"And now you're being childish."

Her temper flared, requiring every ounce of discipline to keep from screaming at him. "Are you trying to work this out or to prove that you're being completely unreasonable? Hand over the keys, Micah."

Micah took them out of his pocket and dropped them into her hand. She was trembling when she took them from him, and her eyes were bright with unshed tears when she looked back at him.

"Don't you ever, ever leave without me. You hear?"

He nodded and took a step toward her. She backed up an equal step.

"Rachel, c'mon," he pleaded. He'd thought he'd been scared yesterday when Andy had disappeared. That was nothing compared to the fear that had scraped his insides raw over the last hour.

This argument had gotten way out of hand, and the open pit in the middle of his stomach was reminding him how scared he'd been that he couldn't find her.

He'd been sick with the idea that Graden had her. Micah knew exactly who to talk to about putting her in this situation—the man who stared back at him from his own mirror every morning.

He couldn't stand the idea of her being hurt, and he dreaded the instant when he'd have to leave her for good. But he'd have to. His life would be no good for her, no matter how much he wanted her in it.

Wrapping her fist around the keys, she backed up another step. "I am so mad at you. It's been a long time since anyone called me childish. I don't think I want to talk to you right now."

"What else is new?" A new flash of anger made him yell. He threw his hands up, somehow aware he was being just as unreasonable as she had accused him of being but unable to let go of the ire and needing to goad her until she was just as upset as he was. "Your life is falling to pieces, and not once in six months do you say one word. Not one. And I find out by accident."

That was closer to what was riding him, he decided with an annoying flash of insight. Not that she'd disappeared this evening, but that she'd been in pain and in trouble for months, and he hadn't known about it. If having her be mad at him was the only way to keep her talking to him right now, he'd take it. The idea that she could order him to leave and it could be the end—he couldn't stand the thought.

She slammed the keys onto the counter and turned to face him just as he had hoped she would, fury in her eyes.

Pointing that finger at him once more, she advanced on him. "I didn't tell you—" she poked in the middle of his chest "—because you betrayed me." Poke. "Because you left without a backward glance as though I was no more important than…" She waved a hand, at a loss for words, while a single tear grew and grew before welling out of her eye and sliding like heartbreak down her cheek. "Like…I wasn't important at all. And now, I'm just the means to get to Graden."

"You're not." The anger drained out of him, and he reached for her, pulling her to him, tucking her cheek close to his and inhaling the scent and warmth of her. "I'm sorry," he said.

Against his back, her fists hit feebly once on each side, and then she shuddered, wrapping her arms around him.

"You left me." The sharp hurt in her voice wounded him.

"I'm sorry," he repeated, the words too puny to convey what was in his heart. "Don't you know that I would never stop looking for you?"

He longed to tell her that he loved her, that he cherished her, that he wanted to spend his life with her. But to make such a confession now wouldn't be right. She'd undoubtedly think he was driven by guilt…and he was …or fear…and he was.

All he could do then was kiss her, which he did, doing his best to convey how precious she was to him.

"Oh, good, you've made up," came Erin's voice from behind him.

Within his arms, Rachel tried to pull back, but he held her fast.

"I'm going to bed," Erin said. "This has been a rough day."

Amen to that, Micah though, once more pressing his cheek against Rachel's and holding her, because to let her go was unthinkable.

FOURTEEN

"We're pulling the surveillance off Graden in Aspen," Flannery Kelman told Micah over the phone the following morning. "We got a break in the Salgado investigation last night, and we need the rest of the team in place for that operation."

"You've got to be kidding me. You know what I'm up against. This is all going to go down today. I need all the manpower we planned for." Micah had just arrived at the Iron Mountain Tram station where he was in his tourist-with-no-taste disguise. He had taken shelter from the rain under one of the wide eaves of the building.

"Tough break," Kelmen replied. "I've also pulled the two agents who've been watching Graden's place."

"Even though you know there's a link between Graden and Salgado."

"Even though," Kelman agreed. "We've got Salgado nailed with or without the connection to Graden, and since that dries up a major network, that's where the resources are going."

Micah's frustration surfaced. "This is in play, and

you're just now notifying me that you've gutted my team?" Rachel was due to arrive any minute, and Erin had taken the tram to the top of the mountain with a staff member a half hour ago.

"You know this happens sometimes," came Kelman's calm voice through the phone while Micah surveyed the nearly deserted parking lot. The day was cold and overcast, and rain had been spitting all morning. The bad weather and the fact that the first tram ride wasn't scheduled for another hour meant not many people were around. Given Kelmen's change in plans, that was the only good news.

"If you and Asher can't handle a simple grab with this money exchange," Kelmen added, "then suspend the operation."

"You did get my briefing last night, didn't you? The one telling you that Erin's cover has been blown and that Graden sent a pair of thugs after Tommy Manderoll, and we still don't know all the reasons why. Graden has to be expecting a setup. There's no way this is going to be a simple grab."

"Then you'll deal with it. The other case is a priority. Suspend the operation for a few days." With that, Kelmen disconnected the call.

Suspend the operation. Given that he had no resources, Micah didn't see any other choice.

Inwardly fuming, he called Erin to let her know. Only, she wasn't answering her cell phone. Since they had made a test run yesterday and communication had worked then, he didn't like any of the possible reasons why she wasn't answering.

He looked up at the mountain where the clouds hung so low the cable for the gondolas disappeared within a hundred feet. The dense clouds, he decided, could be part of why he couldn't raise Erin. Cell phone communication was dicey everywhere in the mountains, more so on days like today.

A moment later, Rachel's car turned into the parking lot from the street. The plan had been for her to head for the gift shop and ticket station. But, since both were still closed and since he had only himself to keep watch over her, he didn't want her in the open.

He headed for her car while the rain began to fall harder. She parked the vehicle, but didn't get out. He figured she didn't want to be in the cold rain any more than he did. When her gaze lit on him, her expressive face registered worry then her recognition of him. She leaned across to the passenger seat and unlocked the door.

Micah opened it and slipped inside.

"It's sure a miserable morning," she said.

"And it's not getting any better," he returned. "Kelmen has reassigned the team."

"What does that mean, exactly?" she asked.

"It's just you, me, and Erin. Not enough for this to be a clean takedown, assuming Graden even shows up."

"So now what?"

He took off the baseball cap, which was dripping with water, and set it on the floor between his legs. "We go home, regroup and do this another day."

She gave him an incredulous look. "That's how this kind of stuff works? Do the bad guys follow the same rules? 'Oh, we don't have the right players on the team today, so we're just going to go home.'"

He grabbed her flailing hand. "I know how this looks."

"I'm just sick of it, Micah." She pressed her free palm against her forehead. "This was supposed to all be over. I didn't sleep last night, and this morning I was so nervous I thought I'd throw up, and now you're telling me that we have to go through all this again on some other day?"

"Unfortunately, yes." Since this operation had become personal, the ups and downs of it had bothered him, too, so he understood what she was feeling. This was one of the many reasons he'd give his right arm to have her safely tucked away with her children. "I'm sorry."

They stared at one another a long moment, and he repeated, "I'm sorry. I am."

The tension in her expression eased, and she managed a smile, squeezing his hand. "I know. Where's Erin?"

"I sent her to the top of the mountain since there were supposed to be two other agents to help down here, and I wanted someone with eyes on at the top, just in case. And, since we knew her cover was blown, I didn't want her hanging around the station where she might be recognized."

Rachel sighed. "I'd never before thought about all the logistics involved with what you do. If it's this complicated for one tiny piece of your war on drugs, the rest of it must be a nightmare."

"Without good planning, it can be," he agreed. The lack of good planning exactly explained the pickle they were in now, and once more he wanted to kick himself for letting things go this far.

"What next, Micah?"

"I need to get Erin back down here, and then we go home." Hoping the cell phone reception had improved, he dialed Erin's number once more. It rang without being answered. He looked over at Rachel, "Since she's not answering, I've got to go get her. I don't suppose I could talk you into riding the gondola with me?"

"With my already queasy stomach?" She shook her head. "Sorry, no. I think I'll go home."

He sat there a moment, thinking about that. He didn't like the idea of her being here alone or at home alone, either. At least there, she had the alarm system.

"Okay, then. I'll see you back at the house."

"Okay."

He got out of the car, watching while she waved, then drove off. He ran back through the rain to the tram station. He had the gondola all to himself as he rode to the top, a trip that took less than ten minutes. He could imagine the views in nice weather would be something, but all he could see after the first hundred feet was fog.

At the top, he found Erin keeping watch from the sheltered entrance to the restaurant.

"What in the world are you doing here?" she asked. After he explained about the change in resources, she shook her head. "Something is mighty fishy about this."

Micah agreed, but there was no point in saying so, not until he had all the facts.

By the time they rode the tram back down the mountain, the weather had taken a turn for the worse, cold rain poured from the sky and it continued to fall for the entire drive back to Rachel's house.

It was locked up tight, and Erin used her key to let them in.

Rachel wasn't there.

Nor was her car in the garage.

Nor did she answer the cell phone.

"Maybe she left a message," Erin suggested. "Maybe she couldn't get through the same way you couldn't reach me."

"Maybe," he agreed, dialing the voice-mail number. Except there was no message.

He closed his eyes. *What am I missing?* He wasn't sure if the plea was a prayer or a cry into the wilderness. Either way, he wished to the depths of his soul that he hadn't left Rachel to drive home alone.

"Is there any chance she went to the grocery store?" Erin asked. "Or maybe she decided to go to church."

"She was coming home." He was positive about that. "But, let's go check, anyway."

He scribbled a note to her and left it in plain sight in the middle of the table, asking her to call when she came in. Then, they headed to the grocery store. Rachel's car was nowhere in sight.

His fear for her safety simmered like acid through his veins, each minute feeling like ten.

Leaving the grocery store, he tried calling again,

and, as before, the phone rang without being answered. Ten minutes later, they arrived at the church. He didn't expect that her car would be here, either.

But there it was, at the end of the row.

Micah couldn't have been more stunned to see her modest sedan if it had somehow turned into a BMW.

He parked the Wrangler next to it. He and Erin went around Rachel's car, peering through the windows and tapping the trunk. Not allowing himself to imagine what he might find inside it, he retrieved his tools from his vehicle, and within seconds opened the trunk. It was empty except for a set of jumper cables and an almost bald spare tire.

Empty. Thank God.

"Well, that's a relief," Erin said from next to him. "What now?"

He had a moment's relief before the bile in his stomach leaked a host of new worries. "We go inside and check."

Though everything looked normal on the inside of her car, he opened that, as well. The soft, feminine scent that he associated with her wafted towards him. Everything looked ordinary enough until he noticed that she had left the bag containing the drop money. He opened it, and the money was still inside, as was her wallet. The cell phone he had given to her was gone, though. None of it gave him a clue about where she might be or why she didn't answer the phone when he called again.

Every instinct made Micah think that Graden had her, but what made no sense was that he would have taken her and left the money behind. For an instant he wondered if she'd done something like last night's encounter with the minister, but after the fight they'd had that didn't seem likely. So Micah was left with the conclusion he'd started with—Graden had her.

Ready as he was to head for Graden's palatial estate in Aspen, Micah had to check the church. Unlikely as it seemed that she'd attended services this morning— or at all—without telling him, he had to at least rule out the possibility.

"My gut tells me that he's taken her to his place in Aspen, but just in case I'm wrong, we've got to check inside the church."

"Okay," Erin agreed.

After stowing his tools and Rachel's bag in his car, he opened the glove box and set his service revolver inside, saying, "I know what you're thinking, but I can't go into a house of worship armed."

After a moment, Erin put hers in, as well. "Even though you know the bad guys don't have the same code?"

"Even though," he agreed, locking the glove box, then the vehicle.

Quietly, they slipped into the back of the church and sat down. The sanctuary had enough people in it that Micah knew it was going to take awhile to look from one person to the next, making sure Rachel wasn't among them. In his gut, he knew she wasn't here, but methodically eliminating the possibility was the only thing he could do right now.

"I'm going to go check the Sunday school rooms," Erin whispered next to him.

While visually searching the congregation for Rachel, he nodded his understanding, half listening to the minister's sermon, which strangely enough had to do with Job. Since his trials had been a subject between Micah and Rachel too often over the last few days, he found himself paying greater attention.

"Suffering is not punishment," the minister was saying.

But it sure does feel like that, Micah thought, thinking of all that had happened recently. Instead of hearing the minister's words, Micah found his thoughts drawn to Rachel's father and his story of the spider. The story about its silk being a bigger mass than the spider and Reverend Holt's assertion that each person was more than he knew captured Micah's imagination.

Micah bowed his head. All morning, he had been bargaining with God for Rachel's safety instead of remembering she was with God no matter what happened. She wasn't alone. As for himself, Micah knew his personal task was to reach inside and do what he was trained to do.

Erin slid back into the pew next to him with a whispered, "She's not here."

During the singing of the final hymn, they slipped out and came to a stop a few feet from the church entrance.

"Do you want her car towed to a crime lab?" Erin asked.

"Yeah." That ever-present knot twisted some more. There wasn't any blood that he could see, but a forensic search would be needed to determine if a crime had been committed. Crime. A benign-sounding term for the awful things beginning to haunt him.

Erin made the call while Micah went to Rachel's car and peered inside once more,

"Before we leave, we need to canvas people as they leave the church. Maybe somebody saw something."

"Why do I have the feeling it's not going to be that easy?" Erin asked.

An hour later they were no closer to knowing where she was or what had happened to her, since no one had seen her car arrive. Had she driven here on her own or had the car been brought here by someone else? Was she on foot or a captive somewhere? Was she hurt?

A thousand questions and no answers to still the hollow ache that pounded through the middle of his chest.

"I'm sorry," Smitty Jones said for the seventeenth time, his hands wrapped so tightly around the steering wheel that his gnarled knuckles were white.

"Stop saying that." Rachel sat in the passenger seat of his old truck with her wrists restrained with duct tape. She was still appalled that she had been duped into stopping to help him. He had waved her down a couple of blocks from her house, standing in front of her car, forcing her to stop. Her thanks for that was him holding a gun on her while another man she had never seen before efficiently restrained her and dumped her in the front seat of Smitty's truck before driving off with her car. "You're sorry, and I'm stupid."

He scowled at her. "I am sorry."

"You lured my son away the other day, and it will

be a long time before I can forgive that." She stared through the rain-spattered windshield to the gloomy day outside. Mount Sophris was hidden by the low-lying clouds. Her attention shifted back to Smitty, a man she'd known for years. His behavior made no sense to her. "You could just take me home, you know."

In the pocket of her slacks, she felt the cell phone vibrate and knew that someone, Micah most likely, was trying to reach her.

"No." He shook his head. "You don't understand," he said, his nasal voice more whiny that usual.

"Then explain." She shifted, trying to find a more comfortable position against one of the seat springs that seemed on the verge of poking through the upholstery.

"You know how fond I am of your two kids. Why, that Andy, he's grown a foot since I last saw him, I swear. Still loves his ice cream, that boy."

"He does, but that's beside the point. You lied to him, and you scared me to death."

"Well, now, I guess I should have thought of that."

Did that mean he hadn't? She lifted her bound wrists to her forehead to rub away the ache. "Yes, you should have." A mileage marker came into view for Aspen, which was seven miles away. "Where in Aspen are you taking me?"

"No harm was meant to Andy or his friend," Smitty said, instead of answering her question.

"No harm?" She held her bound arms toward him. "Like this is meant to be no harm?"

"I didn't know he was going to do that, and I'm sorry for it."

"Well, you can undo all this, Smitty, and you know it. Just turn the truck around and take me home. And if you won't do that, get my cell phone out of my pocket so I can call home."

"Can't," he said.

"Won't," she countered.

He turned a fierce gaze on her. "You don't know everything."

"So you've said. And you still haven't explained."

"I saw you with the money," he said. "I did."

"What are you talking about?" Rachel's stomach slide sideways as they took a curve too fast. She knew what money he meant, or at least she thought she did. But she had no idea what he thought he'd seen. "The road could be slick with all this rain. Maybe you could slow down a bit."

He shook his head. "You were with Miss Angela and you were putting things inside the secret drawers inside that big old armoire thing, and you said that nobody would be the wiser." He looked over at her. "You did."

"I don't know what you're talking about." And that was the truth. She did remember the piece of furniture he referred to. But she had certainly never hidden anything inside it, least of all money.

"Don't play dumb with me. I saw you."

"Me?" she asked. "Or someone you thought was me?"

"You," he insisted. "You and Miss Angela. And Mr. Graden said that if I told him where the money was hidden, he'd forget about the—" He stopped talking suddenly while he stared at the winding road. "You don't need to know about that."

"So you're the one who told Graden I had his missing half-million dollars?" The idea of Smitty making such an accusation was incredulous. Smitty had worked for her for years, and though he'd always been a little pixilated, he had a mechanical knack for fixing almost anything. She wouldn't have thought him capable of this kind of lie.

"I did. And so now, I won't be going to jail, and Clara can keep the earrings," he said referring to the nearly hundred-year-old aunt who lived with him.

"The earrings you stole?" From whom? she wondered.

"I didn't steal them," he said, giving her another of his fierce looks. "They were just sitting there on the counter all pretty and such, and Mr. Graden said that his lady friend didn't want them and what was he going to do with pearl and sapphire earrings like that. And blue is Clara's favorite color."

Smitty's story had huge missing pieces, but if Rachel took this at face value, Smitty had stolen jewelry from Graden and then lied to protect himself. She doubted he even understood the enormity of what he'd done.

"And to keep out of trouble, you told him that I had his money?"

He shot her another glare. "Don't you be talking to me like I did something wrong. You're the one in trouble."

That was sure the truth, she thought.

Ahead of them, clouds had lifted enough that the numerous ski runs were visible on the mountains surrounding Aspen, though the rain continued to fall hard.

Next to her, Smitty leaned over the steering wheel, peering through the fogged-up windshield.

His explanation for the money made her sick at heart—a story that he had made up to save himself. Whatever he thought he had seen was a figment of his imagination. And she was as sure as she was sitting here that Simon Graden would never believe her. Somehow, the recovery of the money was personal. Everything that had happened proved that, and it also proved that he wasn't willing to be rational about it.

A short time later, Smitty turned the vehicle off the highway onto one of the winding roads that climbed from the valley floor. The road curled around the hillsides where ostentatious gates and stone pilasters marked the entrance to expensive properties that were mostly hidden from view. More than a mile in, they arrived at closed wrought-iron gates with an ornate *SG* in the center of each one.

Smitty came to a stop and pushed the discreet call button nearly hidden by a flagstone surround. At the buzz, he said, "This is Smitty Jones."

"Do you have the package?"

"No, sir," he said. "But I do have Miss Rachel."

At that, the gate opened, and Smitty drove in.

The driveway went on for a quarter mile, then turned into a circular drive surrounded by aspen trees. The house beyond sprawled elegantly across the land, the surrounding gardens an artful imitation of an idyllic mountain meadow. Beyond the house, the mountains were shrouded in mist. Smitty's old truck couldn't have been more out of place.

One side of a ten-foot-high double door opened and Two-bits Perez, who had been with Graden that day at the church, came through. He opened the passenger door and pulled Rachel out as though she weighed nothing.

"Mr. Graden wants you to park your truck down by the shed," he said. "You're to wait for him there."

Without saying anything to Rachel, he pulled her unceremoniously toward the house while Smitty drove away. Pausing at the custom mat in front of the door, he commanded, "Wipe your feet."

Rachel swallowed the hysteria bubbling in her chest. Here she was tied up with duct tape and the man wanted her to wipe her feet. Surreal.

Equally so was the foyer inside the door, which looked like something out of *Architectural Digest*. The cove ceiling was banded in wood inlay, depicting flying eagles above a mountain range. At her feet was a polished granite floor with seams done in brass.

Simon Graden came forward, elegantly dressed as always, a smile on his face.

"You really are too good to be true," he said pleasantly. "Did you really believe that I wouldn't see through your puny little scheme?" He held out a hand for her purse, which the other man handed to him. "Thank you, Two-bits. Now, if you'll please make sure Mr. Jones is doing as he was asked."

"Sure thing," he said, leaving Rachel and Graden standing in the wide foyer.

Graden patted her pockets, then pulled out the cell phone. "It's time to let Special Agent McLeod know where you are, don't you think?" Without waiting for an answer, he pressed a couple of buttons as though he knew exactly how it worked, then held the phone to her ear.

Micah answered after half a ring. "Rachel, where are you?"

"Tell the man hello," Graden instructed.

"Micah, I'm with Simon Graden."

Whatever Micah's answer, she didn't hear because Graden lifted the phone to his own ear and said, "Nobody double-crosses me. So, here's the way it's going to be, McLeod. I have Rachel. And you have your marked money supplied by the DEA. You will exchange those for unmarked non-sequential twenties. And, since today is Sunday, I'm assuming you may need a little time to accomplish this task, so you have until nine tomorrow morning to call back at this number," he said, never taking his eyes off Rachel. Then he held up a photograph and said to her, "Tell Special Agent McLeod what you see."

As he had that awful day last week, Graden had a photograph of her children, proving he knew where they were.

Her heart pounded so hard it hurt. "It's my children, Micah," she said, her voice strangled. "Riding a horse being led by a man who looks like he might be your father."

"That's right," Graden said, once more putting the phone to his own ear. "You can't be everywhere at once, McLeod. Mess with me in any way, Rachel is dead. Her children, dead. Your parents, dead."

FIFTEEN

At Graden's calm announcement, Rachel cried out and stumbled away from him.

Completely unperturbed by her outburst, Graden put the phone in his pocket, staring at her across the expanse of a priceless Persian rug. "Now, what to do with you for the next twenty-four hours?"

She had told herself she was tired of being a victim, and yet here she was again. Her hands might be tied, it might be raining outside, but she could run. She roughly knew the area, and she could find help. And, if that didn't work, she'd hide. All she had to do was get out of the house. At that, she ran.

The foyer opened onto an enormous great room with floor-to-ceiling windows overlooking a panoramic view of the mountains. A door to one side led outside. Hearing Graden behind her, she headed for the door, praying that it was unlocked.

It was. Pulling the door open, she ran across the wide flagstone patio, dodging the artfully arranged tables, chairs, and a brass fire pit as she headed toward the knee wall.

On the other side of the wall, aspen and spruce trees grew from a twenty-foot drop before continuing ever downward in sharp folds.

She came to a teetering halt, feeling as though she had reached the edge of the earth. She put out her hands to regain her balance and keep from tumbling over the wall.

Behind her, Graden said, "Go ahead. Jump." He still smiled his polite—sinister—smile, but now he had a gun in his hand. "It will save me the trouble of shooting you."

Her heart stopped, then resumed, double-time. "What did I ever do to you?" Of all the things she might have asked, that stupid I-want-life-to-be-fair question wasn't it.

"Besides steal from me?" He pretended to consider for a second. "Lie to me? Attempt to double-cross me?" He waved the gun. "Besides all that?"

"I never stole from you. That was a lie Smitty told to save his own skin."

"Once I thought so, too. But he knows too many details. The liar, Rachel, is you. I think you believed you could direct the DEA's attention away from you by double-crossing me." He tapped his forehead. "Not too smart. I bet you even think there is someone lurking out there who might save you." He shook his head. "They were there, but they're gone, chasing the more important investigation that *I* led them to. So, you're alone until Special Agent McLeod charges in like the white knight he wants to be."

"He won't come. He'll make sure my kids are okay," Rachel said. He'd better. If she lived through this and he chose to rescue her instead of her children, she'd never forgive him.

"Oh, I'm sure he'll be along. A chance to prove to the lovely Widow Neesham she's worth dying for. I don't think he'll give that up." Once more Graden smiled as though they were discussing something ordinary. "And that other agent, the pretty one who was with Tommy the rat. What was her name?"

"Erin," Rachel whispered around the utter terror choking her.

"Ah, yes, Erin. The gutsy young woman who came to Tommy's rescue. Did she tell you she is a DEA agent?"

Rachel shook her head. That was the truth. Erin hadn't needed to tell her because she had already known.

"That's the trouble with those people. Hiding. Lying. Two-bits said he fixed her good, to give you an exact quote." He made a waving motion with the gun. "Back inside, Rachel. We can't stay out here in the rain all afternoon, can we?"

Her legs trembling, Rachel skirted him to go back into the house.

She had just crossed the threshold when he said, "She got what she deserved, you know." He made a sound of disgust. "Those law-enforcement officers, calling themselves Special Agents as though the label somehow makes them smarter. Since you're the daughter of a kindly minister, I bet you even went to her aid. I can see it now. You rushing to the emergency room."

Rachel stared at him, hating that he found her so predictable.

"And then what?"

"We went home."

He shook his head in disbelief, his frown deepening. "You mean, she wasn't admitted to the hospital?"

Rachel shook her head.

"Two-bits assured me that she was taken care of."

Flooded with the awful realization that Graden had intended Erin the same level of harm as Tommy, Rachel hurriedly said, "She has a concussion. And stitches."

"And where is she now?" His ever-present smile gave way to a frown. "She'll be as dead as McLeod if she shows up here."

Rachel sorted through the gradations of truth. "She was gone this morning when I got up, along with her bag."

"Let's hope she's headed back to Denver with her tail between her legs," Graden said with satisfaction. "One less detail to think about. Now tell me what you know about Tommy."

"The last time I saw him," she said, hearing Micah's reminder in her head— *Stick to the truth. Let the person you're talking to draw his own conclusions,* "was at the hospital with injuries severe enough he ought to have been admitted to intensive care."

She looked over her shoulder at Graden, whose face was suddenly red, a vein at his temple throbbing.

"He's not dead?"

"He wasn't the last time I saw him."

Pressing the gun against her back to keep her walking across the room, he said, "Another job left unfinished. Two-bits is proving to be nearly as inept as your friend Smitty. I don't like all these loose ends, and before the day is over, they'll all be tied up."

"Tied up?"

"Don't be obtuse. They'll all be dead."

That's what she was, she realized. A loose end. He intended to kill her, she thought, except the idea simply didn't gel in her head. What could he hope to gain by his awful, awful threats? Now that she thought about it some more, the man didn't sound rational.

"I never had your money," she said.

"Why should I believe you any more than any of the other liars I'm surrounded by?" he asked, then added. "Don't answer that, and stop stalling."

She stopped suddenly and turned to face him. "My children mean everything to me."

"What kind of mother would you be if they didn't?"

"You wouldn't hurt them."

He smiled once more, and this one chilled her to the core. His eyes gleamed as though he was enjoying this. "Not if McLeod does what he is supposed to."

"Everyone always talks about how careful you are. How smart you are. None of this seems careful or smart."

"You're making the gravest mistake to imply that I'm stupid." Once more he motioned with the gun for her to get going. "You fail to see the greater picture," he said, nudging her across the great room. "With McLeod out of the way, his investigation will go down the tubes because there will be no evidence trail. Stop dawdling and open the door, Rachel."

She did, the cold barrel of the gun prodding her through a restaurant-sized, deserted kitchen and into a mud room, through another doorway and down a steep flight of steps. They went through an exercise room and down a hallway, then down another flight of steps. At the bottom, Graden unlocked a door and flipped on a light.

"Inside," he commanded.

The room was a wine cellar, the temperature cool. Besides the bottles of wine, the only furnishings in the room were a table and two straight-back chairs. He pushed her through the door and tossed a blanket in after her.

"Until I can make sure you're of no further use to me, I don't want you coming down with hypothermia."

"Great. Thanks," she said, shivering inside her rain-damp clothes.

"Sarcasm doesn't become you," he said, closing the door and turning off the light.

The room was pitch-black. Disorienting.

Her hands in front of her, Rachel groped for the chair in the middle of the room.

Until you're of no further use to me. The cellar's chill seeped into her, but the numbing cold inside herself came from knowing he planned to kill her with no more regret than squashing a bug.

She sat down, resting her head against her hands. The duct tape itched, and she figured her skin would sting like crazy when it was peeled off. "It would be nice," she said, "If that was my biggest problem."

Oh, how she wanted her children and everyone else to be safe from Graden. Based on what he'd told her, he wanted Micah dead more than he wanted the money. That thought came with a stab of pain. Micah, who had come to help. And look at the price he was going to pay for that.

As she had so many times over the last long months, she found herself thinking about Job's trials. How everything had been taken from him, all in an effort to make him turn his back on God. He hadn't.

But she had.

In the middle of the memory, she could hear Andy's voice telling her that he'd done as she taught him, and he hadn't been scared. They had been at a baseball game in Denver where they had watched the Rockies play. After the game was over, they had become separated, and she had found him with a police officer.

"I did what you told me, Mommy. I 'membered my name and your name and our phone number." He'd beamed at her, so proud of himself. "I knew you loved me 'cause you said to remember that, and to just do what you told me. And it worked. I wasn't scared or anything."

I knew you loved me. Her Father had commanded, love the Lord Thy God. She hadn't done what she had been taught from earliest childhood, and all these months she had felt lost, alone, forlorn. She had failed to do for herself what she had taught her children.

For the first time, she found herself thinking about the end of Job's story. In the end, he had admitted that with his human mind, he couldn't understand all of God's grandeur or purpose. He'd asked for forgiveness, and he'd received it.

And here in this dark cavern of Graden's evil house, Rachel came to the same conclusion. She couldn't know God's total purpose. For the first time in months, she found solace in the silence, and she felt supported.

If she was going to die, she decided, she didn't want to meet God with all the bitterness that she had carried around for so many months.

Her thoughts soared as she imagined her children on their happiest days. *Keep them in your care, Lord, and watch over them. Make sure they know they are not alone no matter what may happen on this day. If they are supposed to grow up without me, let them remember how much I love them, how precious they are to me, how I want only good for them always.*

It had to be that same way with God, she thought. How could His will be for anything other than good? Maybe she didn't understand in the way that her children sometimes didn't. But in this moment she felt as though everything was going to be okay, just as it had been for Job in the end. "Forgive me, Lord," she whispered.

She searched through the dark for the blanket, then wrapped it around herself, sitting on the floor and bracing her back against one of the racks of wine. Warmer, inside and out, she began to relax. She recited the familiar words of the Lord's Prayer, the meaning of each phrase seeping into her soul and giving her comfort.

"Talk to me, Micah," Erin said from the passenger seat as Micah closed the cell phone.

He heard her through a roaring in his ears and a howl of pain that remained locked in the center of his chest. "Graden has Rachel. He knows the kids are at the ranch."

Opening the door of the Wrangler, he stumbled out

and sucked in a gasp of cold air, bracing his hands against the side of the vehicle. Like the brittle shards of his conscience, icy rain pelted him. This was his fault. All of it. For not staying with Rachel. For believing that he was a step ahead of Graden when, in fact, he'd been ten steps behind. For not running the operation through the tried and proven channels. For letting Kelmen talk him into a different plan.

The rain was cold, but inside he was burning up.

He became aware of Erin standing next to him in the church parking lot, holding an umbrella over them, patting him on the back and assuring him they would find Rachel. He knew they would. *But not dead, Lord. Please not dead.*

She held out her hand. "You don't look so hot. Why don't you let me drive?"

He met her compassionate gaze, then gave her the keys. After they were underway, he dialed Nico's number, and once more the call failed. Finally he looked at the display for the signal strength and found it was nearly zero.

"Technology," Erin sympathized.

"Yeah." Micah looked out at the ever-falling rain. "Where is a gorgeous, clear sky when you really need it?" Then he filled her in on the part of Graden's conversation she hadn't heard. His worry mounted and came with a prayer that he hadn't put his parents in danger. He'd been selfish, he admitted. True, he had wanted everyone safe, but he had also wanted his parents to meet Rachel's children. He wanted them to love the children the way he did. And, he kept hoping that Andy and Sarah would fall in love with his home.

After Erin and Micah returned to Rachel's house, he called the ranch, reaching only the phone-answering machine with his dad's cheerful voice. Nico wasn't answering his cell phone, either, which increased the tension. While Micah was making those calls, he saw that Erin was on the cell phone.

"It's not the best signal," she said, "but it's ringing through to Kelmen."

Micah held out his hand for the phone.

"Things have gone down the tubes here," Micah said when Kelmen picked up, then related the conversation with Graden. "Before you pulled the surveillance, did we get any intel?"

"I can have the agent call you," he said.

"You do that," Micah said. "Any chance you can send them back?"

"None. My takedown is Tuesday morning, and we need every minute to plan the scenarios."

"None," he repeated, feeling his temper slip. "I thought you told me your operation was happening tonight. If you've moved it out to Tuesday, there's time. Is this team in Aspen?"

"You know I can't tell you that over an open line," Kelmen said.

"I'll take that as an affirmative," Micah said, his thoughts racing. "Give me five people, and I'll be done with this by the time it gets dark tonight."

"You can't know that for sure," Kelmen said. "You don't even know for sure where Graden is and where he's taken Rachel."

Micah didn't bother to remind him that he would

have known if the surveillance hadn't been pulled. "Have Sam Freeman call me ASAP," Micah said, naming one of the agents who had been in place for the stakeout, then disconnecting the call.

"Graden has given us a window of opportunity," Micah said to Erin. "Does he honestly think I can't prove he's bluffing about the kids? As for Rachel, he has to have taken her to his house."

"Are you sure?" Erin asked.

After a moment's thought, he nodded. "Everything we know about his organization is that it's small. His primary function was money-laundering for the Salgado organization." Micah snapped his fingers. "He's proven he's manipulative. I don't think it's an accident that Kelmen has pulled the team to go after something bigger in that organization. It feels just like last spring when the investigation against Graden dissolved in a puff of smoke."

"Except this time, he has Rachel."

"Yeah." Which meant it was no longer just business, but as personal as it could get.

Just then the phone rang. Sam Freeman confirmed they had watched Graden's house until Kelmen had pulled them off shortly after dawn this morning. Graden himself hadn't been away from the house except to go to dinner in Aspen a couple of times, and as near as they could tell, the staff at the house was thin. A housekeeper, a groundsman who wasn't there every day, and Two-bits Perez were the only regulars.

The house was secluded. The wooded lot didn't have much level ground, and the house had been built at the edge of the slope to maximize the views.

As they spoke, Micah began formulating a plan. His hunch Graden had taken her to the house had to be right. As soon as Micah could confirm things in Wyoming were fine, he'd pay Graden a visit. The briefing ended with a final warning that cameras monitored the perimeter of the house.

When Micah floated the theory that the other agents were being sent on a wild goose chase orchestrated by Graden, Sam thought it made sense.

"Getting pulled from this operation and leaving you high and dry didn't make sense. We'll meet you at Graden's house. Ward and Jacobs will be with me, too."

"This is going to cause trouble with Kelmen," Micah felt compelled to warn even though he was grateful for the help.

"He'll get over it," was Sam's philosophical reply. "What time do you want us in place?"

They talked a while longer, settling on four-thirty, which gave them all time to assemble equipment and get to the house.

As soon as the call ended, Micah filled Erin in on the plan and placed the calls to send a team to check on the ranch, since he still was unable to reach Nico. He knew Rachel was counting on him to see to her children's safety before coming after her. While he was making calls, Erin had been on the computer, pulling up a weather report. "It's storming there, too," she told him. "So maybe that explains why communication is so bad today."

"Let's hope this storm lifts by the time we get to Graden's. We need every advantage," Micah said.

* * *

By the time Micah and Erin arrived at the turn-off that led up a steep road to Graden's house, the storm was indeed showing signs of letting up, patches of blue sky visible above the clouds. Here and there, ribbons of fog hugged the crevices of the mountains.

A last call to the ranch still got through only to a phone-answering machine, and as he had each time before, he left a message. Then he called Nico's number. On the third ring, Nico answered.

The connection was so bad, most of what Nico told him was garbled, and only about every fifth word came through. Micah couldn't make any sense of the conversation, hung up, dialed again, and wasn't able to get through.

"It's good news that he answered," Erin said.

A final call to the surveillance agents in Wyoming wasn't picked up, either.

A few hundred yards from the entrance to Graden's driveway, a large van was parked off to the side of the road, mostly hidden by a thick copse of aspen trees that grew to within five feet of the edge of the road. Sam and the rest of the team were here, Micah confirmed with a radio check.

"Are you ready for this?" he asked Erin. They had discussed the plan in detail during the drive.

"Now that we know our team is here, I'm good." She returned from where she had hidden on the floor of the back seat.

They headed up the winding road, passing the gated entrances to several other properties before reaching

Graden's. "This has gotta be the place," Micah said for Erin's benefit. "He's got his initials on the gate, and I'd bet it's gold leaf covering them."

He rolled down the window and pressed the call button.

"State your business," a crisp voice finally said.

"I'm here with your money," Micah said. "Send Rachel out, and you can have it."

As expected, the ornate iron gate opened.

SIXTEEN

"What am I doing?" Rachel said to herself, opening her eyes and peering into the dark. *I'm tired of being a victim.* Sitting here, waiting passively for someone else to decide her fate? Was she crazy?

She lifted a hand to wipe her face and realized they were still taped together, the tape smooth against her face. She had forgotten her hands were bound, which made her think that perhaps she had slept. She wondered for how long, though she had the sense that it couldn't have been more than a few minutes.

She had a vague recollection of hearing a couple of loud pops that had sounded like firecrackers. Gunfire? she wondered. Something else? Or maybe she just thought she'd heard something. She cocked her head to the side, listening intently. All she could hear was the sound of her own breathing.

The tape around her wrists really was annoying, she decided, rubbing the tape against her face. *Her hands were taped together.* Something about that idea snagged her attention.

Taped.

Not handcuffed.

Lifting her wrists to her mouth, she tried to grab the edge of the tape with her teeth. Once. Twice. Again, and again. Many tries later, she at last grabbed hold of a tiny edge of tape and pulled. At the first millimeter rip of the duct tape, her heart leaped.

Thank you, she thought, *oh God, thank you.* She was going to at least get her hands free.

Clearly, it hadn't occurred to Graden that she might get loose. Another testimony to her reputation of never making waves, of being the good girl who always did what was expected of her, she thought with a wave of irritation. She had figured out how to free her hands. That was the important thing.

Finally the tape tore free, and she pulled her hands apart. With the return of circulation they tingled, then burned. She welcomed the sensation as she stood up.

Now that her eyes had adjusted to the darkness, it didn't seem quite so black to her. From beneath the door a sliver of light stretched ghostly fingers across the floor, revealing the grout line of the tile. Another paper-thin crack of light showed on either side of the door. She made her way across the small room, knowing this would be too easy if the door were unlocked. It held fast when she twisted the knob, pushed then pulled.

Wondering if there was a key or some other way to unlock the door, she felt all around the handle without getting any sense of it having a lock from the inside. She would have been happy for a light switch, but that wasn't on the inside of the room, either.

After what seemed forever to her, she discovered hinges on the door. She could feel some kind of design embossed along the knuckles that held the pins. A decorative finial was at each end. She pulled…and the pin easily came easily out. She smiled.

An advantage of wealth—the best that money could buy, including a high-end hinge built for decoration and smooth operation rather than security.

"Thank you, Lord," she whispered as the other two pins came out as easily as the first.

The door, of course, didn't budge at all when she pushed on it.

Getting the door dislodged from its hinges might not be all that easy she decided, pressing her ear against the cool wood and listening. She couldn't hear a sound on the other side.

"What next? Think."

Graden had brought her down two long flights of stairs, and though they'd been in a hallway, she'd had a sense of natural daylight, which suggested to her that maybe—she hoped with all her heart—there was an exterior door somewhere that led outside.

Her heart suddenly pounding in anticipation, she began pulling on the hinges, tugging with every bit of her strength. At long last, the door shifted, dropping a mere eighth of an inch. She snatched her fingers out of the way to keep them from being pinched.

Working the door up and down, in and out, it took her a long time to shift it another fraction of an inch. The activity warmed her, and the tiny room no longer seemed so cool.

Finally, the door slipped enough that she could get her fingers between it and the door jamb. She pulled the heavy door toward her. Wood cracked where the locked latch gave way. Afraid of the noise she'd made, she stopped for an instant to listen. She couldn't hear anyone coming down the stairs, and so resumed the task, hurrying now that freedom seemed within her grasp. Finally, she was able to pull the door far enough into the room that she could slip through.

From the outside, she could see that the oak sill next to the latch had come loose from the wall though the lock had securely held. She peeked out of the wine cellar.

Sure enough, at the end of the hallway was a window whose view was filled with white and black aspen trunks. Next to the window was a door. Elation sang through her veins. Freedom was just a few feet away.

Reaching back into the room for a bottle of wine to use as a club, she hurried toward the exterior door, looking back in the other direction to where she could see the bottom of the steps that led upstairs.

The thicket of aspen outside the door would provide her with a hiding place while she got her bearings and decided what to do next. She reached for the door handle and twisted it. It moved, but the door didn't pull open. Above the handle was a lock, one that required a key to open the dead bolt. She studied it a moment, forcing herself to think clearly.

One more obstacle, she thought. She'd rather go through the door, though using the wine bottle to break the window was tempting. Looking around, it made sense to her that a key had to be hidden somewhere close by. This door was a long way from upstairs, and it would be a pain to go all the way back up there to get a key. She reached for the thin ledge of the frame above the door, thinking that's where she'd hide a key. To her surprise, her fingers brushed across a key, dusty, as though it had been there a long time.

The door opened without a sound, and it didn't set off any alarms. So far, so good.

She pulled the door closed behind her and stood a long moment, so thankful to be out of the house, so thankful to be breathing in fresh air. Did she lock the door or not? Graden would immediately see that she had escaped. Deciding that locking the door might slow him down enough to give her some advantage, she secured the dead bolt, then pocketed the key.

The air was chilly, but smelled crisp, the way it always did after rain. Above the canopy of aspen, she could see the clouds weren't as black as they had been earlier. One more thing to be thankful for, she decided. She didn't have to traipse through the woods in the rain, though she'd still be wet from the water clinging to the underbrush.

She made her way to the edge of the house, then peered around the corner. There, the slope gave way to a level area where there were a couple of outbuildings, one looking like a barn and the other a large prefabricated shed. Next to the barn, she saw Smitty's truck and remembered Two-bits' instructions for him to drive down here. Then Graden had sent Two-bits down here, which had to mean they were close by.

She stood there a long time trying to decide what to do next. No way did she want to get caught again. But, Smitty's truck was transportation, and that seemed a lot better idea than heading back to the highway through the woods. Darkness would fall soon. And though she was confident about her sense of direction, wandering around in the woods at night wouldn't be her smartest move.

Finally, she ventured toward the closest of the two buildings, using the trees for cover. When less than ten feet separated her from the building, she hurried across the open ground and peered in the window. Gardening tools, and a small tractor were inside the building. Not seeing anything else, she edged toward the trees separating it from the other building close to where Smitty's truck was parked.

Once more, she had to cross open ground before reaching it. She hurried to the truck and peered in, hoping that he had left the keys in the ignition. No such luck. Nothing about this had been easy, she thought, so why would this be?

Bending over and using the truck for cover, she headed toward the building, thinking about how quiet it was. Not even birds were chirping, which seemed a little unusual to her. She couldn't decide if the silence was because it had been raining or was due something more sinister.

The other building was a garage, she realized, when she peeked in. A sixties-era muscle car of some kind was inside and looked as though it was being rebuilt, since it was covered with gray primer paint and the hood was missing. From her vantage point, she could see it had no engine.

No keys for Smitty's car and no other transportation except for the tractor in the shed. Deciding she didn't have any choice but to head through the woods to find help, she came around the corner of the building.

Lying in the long, wet grass were two men.

Stifling a startled yelp, she looked back toward the house. Not seeing movement, she crept closer to get a better look.

Smitty, with his eyes wide open and Two-bits, curled on his side.

And both of them clearly dead.

Micah drove in a quarter of a mile through an aspen grove, gold leaves covering the black pavement in an abstract mosaic. Micah slowed the vehicle, and Erin opened the passenger door, slipping out of the car, instantly disappearing into the underbrush.

"Be safe," came Erin's warning through Micah's earpiece. Then a second later. "Would you look at this house. I've seen country clubs that were smaller."

Micah made the last turn, and the stone-and-cedar house came into view. The natural landscape set off the house to perfection.

"Just a little cabin in the mountains," he agreed.

The front door stood wide open, but no one was in sight. Micah prayed they had picked the right spot for Erin to get out of the car without being seen. "I'm here," he said for her benefit, putting the vehicle into Park and shutting off the ignition.

"We've got your back," came Sam's reassuring voice through the earpiece. "Graden is armed and waiting just inside the door."

Micah opened the door of the Wrangler and stood, the body of the car shielding him from the open door.

A man stood inside, just as Sam had said, barely visible in the shadows.

"Mr. McLeod," the man said pleasantly, lifting a handgun toward him. "Put your hands on the top of the car where I can see them, please."

Doing as requested, Micah said, "I figured you'd be as anxious as me to have this all behind us." This was the opening gambit for the game of cat and mouse that would require every ounce of his patience.

"That must have been some very cooperative bank you found, to have my money already."

"Fortunately, I have connections," Micah agreed. "Send Rachel out. Let's make the exchange, and this will be the end of it."

"Indeed it will be the end," Graden said, still in the shadowed entryway. "I knew you would come, that you'd choose saving her over saving her children."

"You don't have them," Micah said. "Nor can you get to them." He wished he knew for sure, but he put every ounce of confidence he had into the statement, his gaze locked with Graden's. "I've spoken with my agent on the ground. They're all safe and sound."

"You're that positive of Nico's loyalty?"

"I am." That Graden knew his first name came as a surprise, but Micah made sure that he didn't so much as blink, much less flinch. When this was over, he'd have to find out if there had been any contact between the two.

"Did you come alone?" Graden asked.

"Do you see anyone with me?" Micah countered. "Why play this game? You won't believe me if I tell you I'm alone."

Graden smiled as though he held the winning hand. "I do know the stakeout you had watching the house is gone. Don't bother denying they were here. I know they were."

"Send Rachel out," Micah repeated.

"Why don't you bring the money in and come with me to get her?"

This was what he'd been hoping for, but Graden would suspect he wasn't alone if he agreed too quickly. "That puts me in a bad position. I'll wait here."

Graden came closer to the open door, holding the weapon with the assurance of a man who had been trained and wasn't afraid to use it. "You'll retrieve the money, McLeod, and you'll come with me."

"It's in the very back of the vehicle," Micah said.

"Then get it out. And I want your hands where I can see them at all times."

"I don't have a clear shot," came a voice through the earpiece. "Can you get him outside a little more?"

Micah moved toward the back of the Wrangler, his hands in the air. "I've been curious about what led you to Rachel," Micah said. "We all know she wouldn't steal."

Graden smiled. "But you thought so. You see, everything that Two-bits Perez told you, he told me."

Micah had wondered for months if Two-bits hadn't

been feeding information to the other side. He wished he could deny that he had been suspicious of Rachel, even though he recognized the baiting statement for what it was.

"Stop stalling and get the money out," Graden said, "or I'll shoot you where you stand."

Micah rolled down the rear window of the vehicle and reached in for the briefcase. The shotgun caught his gaze, and he longed to reach for it, instead.

"Don't even think about reaching for the weapon I know you've got back there," Graden said, as if reading his mind.

Micah held up the briefcase.

"Good." Graden stepped back into the shadow of the house. "You'll come into the house now."

Micah followed him, and the instant they were inside, Graden commanded him to shut the door. Micah did, while Sam's reassuring voice came through his earpiece. "No worries. We'll be in the second you're cleared from the door.

"It's your show," Micah said to Graden. "Where to?"

"Take off the jacket and hat. Let's make sure you're not armed, first."

Shrugging out of the jacket, Micah let it slide to the floor and set his hat on top of it. Graden would see his shoulder holster, would be expecting that. He might even be expecting the one at the small of his back, but if Micah was lucky, he wouldn't look for the second one hidden under his shirt. So far, Graden hadn't noticed the nearly invisible earpiece that kept Micah in communication with the team.

"Set the shoulder holster on the floor. The one at your back, too. Nice and easy," Graden commanded.

Micah complied, asking, "So, where is Two-bits?"

"Out back," Graden said. "And I think you'll be very pleased to see what I've done with him."

"I'm headed down the side of the house," came another agent's voice into Micah's ear. "I'll check it out."

"Open the briefcase," Graden ordered.

Micah did, turning it around so Graden could see the neatly banded stacks of twenties.

"You must think I'm stupid," he said. "Any fool can see about half of the money is missing."

Micah shrugged. "I figure I needed a little insurance. We'll get the rest of it where I left it hidden in the woods after I have Rachel."

"Rachel," Graden sneered. He pulled the trigger, once. Twice. The first round hit the top of his shoulder, and the second caught him square in the middle of his chest.

The sound of a gunshot from the house made Rachel whirl around.

Two men stood directly behind her, their guns leveled toward her. From inside the house more shots sounded, and someone screamed, then one more shot.

She'd heard the phrase about life flashing before her eyes, and she understood as the images from hers flew through her mind. Her father, Sarah, Andy.

"Rachel Neesham?" one of them questioned,

lowering his weapon. And then she noticed the initials DEA emblazoned in large letters across the cap he wore.

From somewhere, she found her voice. "You're—"

"Micah sent us," the other one said. "Samuel Freeman at your service, ma'am." He reached toward her. "I don't think you'll be needing that wine bottle."

Slowly she lowered her arms, just then realizing she'd been holding the bottle like a club. She began to shake as she let him take the bottle. "The gunfire…" Then she pointed toward the grass behind her. "Those men…"

"Rachel?" Erin burst into view. Like the two men, she wore a dark jacket announcing that she was DEA. She closed the distance between them and hugged her. "Are you okay? We've been so worried about you."

"I'm fine," Rachel said, grabbing Erin's arms. "Graden threatened my children. Are they okay?"

When she didn't immediately answer, Rachel was reminded of all those times when Micah had weighed what he was going to say without telling her the whole truth. A mass of despair curdled in her stomach, and she felt her chin quiver.

"Don't you dare tell me they're—" She couldn't even say the words.

Erin shook her. "We don't know, Rachel. Because of the storm, we've had a terrible time with communication."

"No."

Erin pulled her close and whispered. "Trust Micah. He wouldn't have come here if he'd thought there was any chance your children were in harm's way. He wouldn't."

"You don't know if they're okay, but you came here

anyway?" Rachel wanted to scream her frustration. This wasn't how it was supposed to be. "Let's call—"

"Micah's been shot," the agent next to Erin suddenly announced, sprinting toward the house.

The color drained out of Erin's face, and Rachel went completely numb, her legs somehow carrying her toward the basement door she had come out of a few minutes earlier. It turned out that she didn't need the key for the door because the two agents used a battering ram to open it.

They ran up the two flights of stairs. Several other agents were in the kitchen, two of them kneeling next to a prone form.

Rachel pushed her way through, and Micah lay in the center of room, his shirt pulled off and a Kevlar vest on the floor next to him. She couldn't get a good look at him because of the men surrounding him, but she learned he was going in and out of consciousness, which had the other agents worried.

Finally she was able to squeeze through, dropping to her knees next to him. Blood was everywhere.

"McLeod, talk to me, buddy," one of the agents said. "You're scaring the pretty girl here waiting for you to wake up."

She had no conscious realization of taking his hand, but knew that she had when she felt his fingers grasp hers.

"Micah?"

At the sound of her voice his eyes opened. Tears sprang into hers, streaming down her face.

"Is he going to be okay?" she asked.

"The bullets didn't hit anything serious," the agent explained. "Caught him high on the shoulder. He's lucky. Missed his lung, missed bone." He pointed to a red mark over Micah's heart. "The Kevlar vest did its job."

He could have died. *Oh, dear God,* she thought. He could have died. Only he hadn't. Once more that prayer of gratitude filled her.

His eyes opened, his gaze intent on hers. "I'm sorry," he croaked.

She didn't know what he could possibly be sorry about. He'd come to save her and, in the process, had nearly gotten himself killed.

"I am so mad at you," she whispered, squeezing his hand hard. She didn't like that he'd put his life on the line for her. Worse, she hated the knowledge that he faced this same kind of danger in his job all the time. Despite what she had intellectually known about the dangers, she had failed to consider he was putting his own life in danger for hers. No amount of gratitude could ever repay that.

"I know. I should have waited until I knew your children were okay," he croaked.

Micah pulled his hand away, closing his eyes against the pain that he saw in Rachel's. He couldn't blame her for being angry, especially since he didn't yet know for sure that her children were okay.

"No," she said, her voice anguished while he was loaded onto a gurney and wheeled out of the house. "Micah, that's not what I meant."

Tears were streaming down her face. He vowed this would be the last time he made her cry.

SEVENTEEN

"Miss," another paramedic said, guiding Rachel toward the kitchen and away from Graden's sheet-covered body, "let's check you out and make sure you're good to go."

The gurney carrying Micah continued on, and his gaze lost contact with Rachel when someone stepped between them.

By the time they reached the foyer, he became aware that his cell phone was ringing. With all the chaos, no one else seemed to hear it.

"Can somebody get my phone out of my pocket?" he asked. One of the paramedics retrieved it and handed it to him. When Micah saw Nico's name on the display, he breathed a sigh of relief. "Tell me good news, buddy," he said.

"Good news, huh?" came the younger agent's cheerful voice over the line. "The storm is over, and the linemen just left after replacing the transformer the lightning took out, and Andy has only a broken arm—no concussion. Is that enough good news for you?"

Despite the pain in his own shoulder, that made

Micah struggle to sit up. "What do you mean Andy has only a broken arm? What happened?"

While Nico explained about being out on a horseback ride when the storm first hit and one of the horses throwing Andy, the EMT pressed Micah's back to the gurney and continued wheeling him toward the ambulance.

"Wait a minute," he ordered as they began loading him. He handed the phone to the EMT. "Give the phone to Rachel. This is a call she needs to have."

"McLeod?"

Micah lifted his head and saw Flannery Kelmen at the double doors of the ambulance. He climbed inside as though he had every right to be there.

"How serious is it?" he asked the EMT.

"I'm right here," Micah said with irritation, "and I'm not unconscious, so talk to me."

Kelmen dropped to a knee next to him. "Since I need to get inside, I'll be brief. My ego got in the way on this one, and that stripped you of your team, left you improvising at the last minute, and from the looks of things, came close to getting you killed." He took a breath. "Any fallout with this debacle—it's all mine, and I'll make sure our superiors know that." He climbed back out of the vehicle, and said to the paramedic closing the door, "Take good care of him."

The doors to the ambulance closed, and Micah stared at the white ceiling, surprised by Kelmen's admission. His thoughts, though, were consumed with Rachel and her family. He was at once thankful the kids were okay and heartsick that he had once again made choices that had betrayed Rachel's trust.

He'd left her alone, which had put her squarely in harm's way.

He'd chosen to come after her before knowing for sure that her children were safe.

She had every right to be angry with him.

The next hours were filled with the monotony of being poked and prodded. His sternum ached from the impact of the gunshot, and the other wound was high on his shoulder, merely a graze, though it had bled like crazy. He knew from experience that he'd feel worse tomorrow than he did tonight. He also knew that he'd be kept overnight for observation.

The fact that he could recite the procedures and the routine gave him pause for thought. He remembered telling Rachel that working undercover was a young man's game. Since he was a solid fifteen years older than Nico and most of the other agents on the team, no way could he call himself a young man. In the middle of thinking about the promotion and desk job that he had been encouraged to apply for, he fell asleep.

He awoke sometime later to a dark room. Make that a hospital room, he decided, taking in the dim lights and the antiseptic smells.

The memory of this afternoon hit him all over again, and he gingerly pressed a hand against the ache in the middle of his chest where the bullet had struck the Kevlar vest. He discovered his shoulder was covered with a thick pad, and a vague recollection of talking to the doctor surfaced. No real damage, and in all likelihood, he could go home tomorrow.

He was grateful for his life and for the team that had

crashed through the door an instant after Graden had fired. And Rachel hadn't been hurt. He remembered that. Another thing to be thankful for.

As if thinking about her conjured more vivid memories, he thought he caught a whiff of her scent within the sharper hospital smells. He twisted his head and saw that she was asleep in the chair next to the bed. And then he realized she was holding his hand.

Love and regret curled through him, settling into their familiar hole in the middle of his chest. He stared at her, memorizing each detail of her softly illuminated face. He was so surprised she was here, even more surprised that she was holding his hand.

As if she had become aware that he was no longer asleep, she opened her eyes, and immediately straightened. "Hi."

"What are you doing here?" he asked, letting go of her hand, mostly to prove to himself that he could.

"Making sure you're okay," she said. "Erin and I have been taking turns watching over you. How are you feeling?"

"Fine." Physically that was true. "It's late. You should go home."

She stood, rearranging the blanket covering him. "I wanted to return your cell phone. And I couldn't go until I knew that you were okay. "

"I'm fine," he repeated. "Graden didn't hurt you?"

"No." She took a breath. "I talked to everyone at your house. Nico's bringing the kids home tomorrow."

"Good. Everything will be back to normal."

"Yes." She plucked at the bed covers as though she

didn't know what to do with her hands. "I talked to your doctor, and he says that the wound in your shoulder isn't serious, and it cleaned up fine. If everything looks normal in the morning, you'll be released then."

"That's about what I figured." He didn't add that he'd been shot before, so he knew the drill. That would only give her something more to worry about, which was one more reminder of his promise to himself. He'd been living in a fantasy world to think they could have a future. Undercover jobs were hard on families, and he couldn't—he wouldn't—ask Rachel to live that kind of life. Even a desk job wasn't immune from the stress.

The silence grew awkward as he stared at her. Everything that had gone wrong over the last ten days had been because he'd let his emotions get in the way, exactly what Kelmen had accused him of. No way should Rachel have been left alone. When the plan had been changed, he should have gotten her to safety. End of story.

"You need to go home," he said, wanting to beg her to stay.

"Will you come by the house tomorrow?" She swallowed. "Andy and Sarah will want to see you."

Much as he'd like to see them, too, doing so wouldn't be fair to any of them. With Graden out of the way, Rachel could have her life back. Her financial worries weren't solved, but her name would be cleared, at least. That was a start. One she deserved.

"I've got to get back to Denver," he said, deliberately sounding dismissive. "Debriefing and paperwork and all that. You know."

"Well." She took a step back and glanced around as though searching for something. "You sleep well, Micah."

The instant she turned and headed for the door, he wanted to call her back, but he managed to resist until she reached the door.

"Rachel?"

"Yes?" Hope filled her voice, her eyes.

"Go with God," he whispered.

"Thanks," she said with a nod, her face hidden in the shadow. "You, too."

And then she was gone. He kept telling himself that it was for the best.

The following afternoon, Nico arrived with her dad and her children. Rachel ran down the steps at the front of her house, embracing them all the instant they were out of the car. The kids had a thousand things to tell her all at once, talking over each other, and vying for her attention.

A neon-orange cast covered Andy's broken arm. "And it glows in the dark," he proudly told Rachel. "Mom, you should see Micah's ranch. He has this horse named Thunder—"

"And there's a really cute colt, too," Sarah interrupted. "And guess what, Mom? That loose tooth fell out last night. See?" She pulled her lip out of the way.

"I think they missed you," Nico said blandly, setting a couple of suitcases on the ground.

"I missed them." Rachel gathered them close into a fierce hug, looking over their heads to her father. "Hi,

Dad." She imagined launching herself into her father's arms the way her children had hugged her.

"How was the trip?" Erin asked, joining them on the sidewalk in front of the house, and picking up one of the bags.

"Long," Sarah said, dragging out the word. "I don't want to sit down for three days."

Erin laughed.

Rachel didn't know what she would have done without Erin's company for the day. Together, they'd cleaned the house and made a big dinner that included a chocolate cake for dessert. Through the activities, Micah's name had come up only once, though he occupied about every other thought in Rachel's head. Erin had told her he'd been released from the hospital and was on his way back to Denver.

That knowledge left a giant void in Rachel, but she determinedly ignored it. She'd survived the man leaving her before, and she could do it again.

Even if she hadn't known she was in love with him the last time he left her.

Even if she couldn't imagine her life without him this time.

Even if she'd been under the mistaken impression that he loved her, too.

"I'm starved," Andy announced, taking a bag of toys that Nico handed him.

"I made your favorite for dinner," Rachel said.

"Hot dogs?"

"Hot dogs are your new favorite? I thought you liked fried chicken."

"*I* do," Sarah said while Andy grinned up at her and said, "I forgot. Chicken *is* my favorite."

Rachel looked past her dad at Nico. "You're invited, too."

"Thanks," he said. "I won't be turning down a home-cooked meal."

"Being around Rachel today has almost made me wish that I cooked," Erin said. "She didn't believe me when I told her that I could get along without a stove or oven. Just give me a microwave."

"You just need someone to cook for," Rachel's dad said.

Erin and Nico, their arms filled with the paraphernalia from the trip, followed the kids into the house, which left Rachel standing on the sidewalk with her dad.

He held out his arms, and she walked into his hug.

"Welcome home, Dad."

"You sound better," he said.

"I am." She let go of him, and looped an arm through his. "I've finally figured out several things."

Covering her hand with his, he said, "I have, as well."

They reached the porch, and she guided him toward the wicker swing that hung to one side.

After they sat down, he studied her in the compassionate way that was so much a part of him. Rachel felt at once vulnerable and as though her dad was seeing her, really seeing her, for the first time in a long while.

He cleared his throat. "I'm sorry I wasn't more considerate of your feelings when I went to visit Angela."

"I know." Sudden tears burned at her eyes. "And I'm sorry I made you think you had to choose between being my dad and being a man of God." She sniffed. "In the last few days, I've figured out that if you change your thinking, then the things you notice are different. I have both you and Micah to thank for helping me realize that my life wasn't all that bad."

"And what about Micah?" he asked.

"He's gone back to Denver," she said, hoping her tone was neutral enough to hide her anguish about that.

She hadn't hidden the pain as well as she wanted though, because her dad turned toward her, grasping her hands within his. "Are you okay?"

"I'm going to be," she said, meaning it. She had survived loss before. She could do it again.

Andy burst out the door, a skateboard under his good arm. "I'm gonna go see if Jeremy can play," he announced coming to a skidding halt in front of them.

Rachel grabbed the skateboard. "Since you have a broken arm, maybe walking is a good idea."

"Mom!"

His plaintive tone made her grin. Things were well and truly on their way to being back to normal.

"Be back in forty-five minutes," she told him.

"Mo-om."

Rachel tousled his hair. "Or stay here until dinnertime. Since you just got home, that might be a good idea."

He grinned. "It might." Turning back toward the house, he said, "Maybe Nico will play catch with me."

"That broken arm hasn't slowed him down much," Rachel said.

"He was sure a trooper when it happened," her dad said. "Scared me to death, but he did just fine. He reminded me of you when you were about that same age and broke your arm."

Surprised and delighted that he had remembered that small thing from so many years ago, Rachel laughed. "Only kid on the block who broke an arm while playing with a hula hoop."

The next hour was chaotic while the kids ran through the house and Rachel finished cooking dinner with Erin's assistance. When they sat down for dinner, Rachel looked around the room, certain she had never been more grateful for the good in her life. They joined hands, and Rachel bent her head, waiting for her dad's deep voice to say grace. He didn't, and she finally looked at him.

His eyes were gentle when they met hers. "I think you should say grace," he said. "Your home, your table."

"Good," Andy said, squeezing her hand. "I like your prayers, Mom."

Smiling, Rachel closed her eyes once more, feeling her daughter's hand on one side and her son's on the other and absorbing the love in the room.

And for the first time in a *long* time, she found the words to express the gratitude in her head.

Taking a deep breath, Micah opened the wrought-iron gate in front of Rachel's big, two-story Victorian house and stepped onto the brick walkway that led to her front door. He squared his shoulders and climbed the steps to the porch, determined to see this through and more scared than he'd ever been in his life.

On his way back to Denver, he'd been rehashing everything they'd said to each other over the last days. The last thing she'd said to him before the ambulance took him away kept sticking in his head—*Micah, that's not what I meant.* If she wasn't mad at him about her children, what had she been talking about? He had to know.

The sun had fallen about an hour ago, and welcoming light spilled from the windows of Rachel's house. The heavy oak door with its oval etched glass stood open, the hallway beyond the screen door was bright and welcoming. He imagined simply opening the door and going inside, but his courage deserted him.

He could hear cheerful voices and the clink of silverware against dishes coming from the dining room.

He rang the bell, the chimes echoing through the house.

"I'll get it, Mom," came Sarah's voice while Andy said, "No, I will."

"Sit, you two," he heard Rachel say. "I'll see who it is."

Micah took off his hat and let his arms drop to his side.

She came out of the dining room, wearing one of those skirts that swirled around her legs, a smile lighting her face. A smile that vanished when she saw him even though she kept walking toward the screen separating them.

"You," she said. She pushed open the door, making him step back slightly. Her eyes shimmered. "Micah, what are you doing here?"

He fingered the brim of the hat, too aware of the other afternoon he had come to her house and of their conversation so far being an echo of that one.

His eyes remaining steady on hers, he cleared his throat. "Last night, when you told me you were mad at me." He took a breath. "What were you mad about?"

"You came back to ask me that?"

He nodded, and she stepped through the door, coming onto the porch, letting the door slam behind her. Her chin was up, and he had the feeling she was still angry. She took a step toward him. He wanted to retreat, but stayed rooted where he stood.

"For getting yourself shot." Another step. "While trying to rescue me." A scant six inches separated them, and her head tilted back.

"That wasn't about the children?"

One tiny shake to her head. "Erin told me about the awful choice you had to make and all the things you did to get help rounded up."

"It could have all been for nothing."

"But it wasn't, was it?" She moved closer, as if daring him to step away. "Why are you really here, Micah?"

Under the porch light, her eyes were wide, brilliant, reflecting the rich greens and browns of life that he liked so much. Her expression was at once as scared as he was feeling and open, as though his answer meant everything to her.

"I'm in love with you," he said, wanting to grab the words back as though doing so would somehow shield his bruised heart.

The shimmer in her eyes spilled over.

"Aw, Rachel, don't cry. Please don't cry."

She put her arms around his waist, stepping even closer, her lovely gaze still locked with his. "Those are tears of relief, Micah McLeod. I was sure you'd left me again."

"Never again," he vowed, pulling her close. "I made it as far as Vail Pass. I had to come back and stay until you kicked me out."

"That won't happen." She pressed a palm against his cheek. "I love you, too."

He kissed her then, the possibilities for their future shimmering within their embrace. He wanted her in his arms for the rest of his life, and he'd make any change required of him to have it.

"Mom, who's here?" Andy asked from inside the house, his footsteps coming toward the door. "Micah! Sarah, come quick. It's Micah!"

The screen door opened to the clatter of the children running, and all at once, they were surrounding him and Rachel, their hugs including him. Him! And he was so bowled over with gratitude he couldn't speak.

"Since you're kissing Mom," Andy said, "does this mean you're gonna marry her?"

He looked down at Andy's and Sarah's expectant faces. "Would that be okay with you?"

"Yep," Andy said while Sarah clapped her hands together and said, "Yes, oh, yes."

Micah's glance came back to Rachel. "Do I need to ask your dad's permission, too, before I ask you?"

That warm smile that he'd fallen in love with months

ago reached all the way to her eyes and into her soul. "I'm pretty sure he'd say it was okay."

"And what about you, Rachel?" he asked, his voice husky. "What do you say?"

She opened her arms, and he stepped into them. "I think it's okay, too."

"Okay?" he said with a laugh, love and anticipation filling the hole in the middle of his chest. "I guess that will have to do."

She rested her head against his heart. "You're not going to argue with perfect, are you?"

He bent his head until it rested against her. "Perfect, hmm. Well, okay, then."

"Does this mean I get a horse?" Andy asked. "I really *need* a horse."

"Do not," Sarah said in the way of big sisters, heading back inside, and holding the door open.

With Rachel tucked close to his side, Micah stepped over the threshold and knew that he'd come home.

* * * * *

Look for Angela's story
FROM THE ASHES
Sharon Mignerey's new novel
Available October 2007
wherever Steeple Hill Books are sold.

Dear Reader,

The idea for this book came to me during big changes in my life. Was it art imitating life or life finding its way into art, since the heroine of this story also faces huge changes? A bit of both, I suspect.

After we had lived in the Denver area for many years and had raised our children there, my husband's work took him to the Texas Gulf coast for a temporary assignment. It soon became permanent, and so we moved. The setting for this book was comforting—a revisit to the part of Colorado where my grandparents lived.

Life cannot stand still, as we are reminded in Ecclesiastes 3:1: "For everything there is a season, and a time for every purpose under heaven." I like the rest of that chapter of Ecclesiastes, as well, since it tells us that joy is ours for the asking.

May the changes that come into your life be for good and always with God.

QUESTIONS FOR DISCUSSION

1. Rachel is a "what you see is what you get" kind of woman who has always followed the rules. Micah often works as an undercover agent, so he keeps much of himself hidden. What are the differences in how they each view the truth?

2. Rachel's children have a high degree of trust in Micah. How warranted is that, and how might a child's instinct about that trust be reinforced?

3. Rachel is at the brink of ruin when the story opens. How much of that comes from the circumstances in her life and how much is from the way she views the world? Besides the story of Job, what are other biblical examples that might have provided her guidance?

4. When Rachel meets Simon Graden and realizes he's behind the escalating threats, what is her reaction? Do her choices seem reasonable?

5. One of the themes of this book is forgiveness. How does it play out in the story? How does this fit with your ideas about forgiveness?

6. Another theme in the book is trust—earning it, regaining it. What events in the story demonstrate Rachel's path from distrust to trust? What are the similarities and differences between Micah, his boss (Flannery Kelmen), and Simon Graden regarding how they earn trust?

7. Bad things do happen to good people, sometimes accompanied by a loss of faith, as happened with Rachel. How does the idea "as you believe, so it is done unto you" apply to her situation?

8. At a key moment in the book, Rachel's father tells Micah a story about a spider spinning a web. In what ways does this idea play out in the rest of the story?

9. Another important theme in this story is taking responsibility for and owning up to the things you've done. What does the Bible say about this?

10. Rachel confesses to Micah that she finds God when she's in nature more than when she's in church. How does this fit with your experiences?

REQUEST YOUR FREE BOOKS!

2 FREE INSPIRATIONAL NOVELS
PLUS 2
FREE
MYSTERY GIFTS

Love Inspired.

YES! Please send me 2 FREE Love Inspired® novels and my 2 FREE mystery gifts. After receiving them, if I don't wish to receive any more books, I can return the shipping statement marked "cancel." If I don't cancel, I will receive 4 brand-new novels every month and be billed just $3.99 per book in the U.S., or $4.74 per book in Canada, plus 25¢ shipping and handling per book and applicable taxes, if any*. That's a savings of 20% off the cover price! I understand that accepting the 2 free books and gifts places me under no obligation to buy anything. I can always return a shipment and cancel at any time. Even if I never buy another book from Steeple Hill, the two free books and gifts are mine to keep forever.

113 IDN EF26 313 IDN EF27

Name	(PLEASE PRINT)	

Address		Apt. #

City	State/Prov.	Zip/Postal Code

Signature (if under 18, a parent or guardian must sign)

Order online at www.LoveInspiredBooks.com

Or mail to Steeple Hill Reader Service™:

IN U.S.A.: P.O. Box 1867, Buffalo, NY 14240-1867
IN CANADA: P.O. Box 609, Fort Erie, Ontario L2A 5X3

Not valid to current Love Inspired subscribers.

Want to try two free books from another series?
Call 1-800-873-8635 or visit www.morefreebooks.com

* Terms and prices subject to change without notice. NY residents add applicable sales tax. Canadian residents will be charged applicable provincial taxes and GST. This offer is limited to one order per household. All orders subject to approval. Credit or debit balances in a customer's account(s) may be offset by any other outstanding balance owed by or to the customer. Please allow 4 to 6 weeks for delivery.

Your Privacy: Steeple Hill is committed to protecting your privacy. Our Privacy Policy is available online at www.eHarlequin.com or upon request from the Reader Service. From time to time we make our lists of customers available to reputable firms who may have a product or service of interest to you. If you would prefer we not share your name and address, please check here. ☐

LIREG07

Love Inspired®
SUSPENSE

TITLES AVAILABLE NEXT MONTH

Don't miss these four stories in April

DANGEROUS SEASON by Lyn Cote
Harbor Intrigue

Sheriff Keir Harding hoped to put his troubled past behind him—until an arsonist threatened his community. Keir enlisted the aid of Audra Blair, but could he ever forgive himself if she paid the ultimate price for getting involved?

THE SOUND OF SECRETS by Irene Brand
The Secrets of Stoneley

The night she found her mother murdered, Nerissa Blanchard was grateful for the quiet strength of Officer Drew Lancaster. But the strange happenings that followed had her wondering if she was losing her mind—or if someone wanted to silence her forever.

NOWHERE TO HIDE by Debby Giusti

Lydia Sloan's husband's killer wanted her son to be his next victim. Fearing for their safety, she fled. She soon realized security guard Matt Lawson was the only one she could trust with her secret and her child's life.

CAUGHT IN THE MIDDLE by Gayle Roper

Newspaper reporter Merry Kramer was horrified to find a dead body in her car. Surrounded by suspects, she'd have to use all her investigative skills to keep from becoming front-page news as the killer's next victim.

LISCNM0307